MOON BLADE

/ / / /

J.R. RAIN

&

MATTHEW S. COX

THE VAMPIRE FOR HIRE SERIES

Published by
Crop Circle Books
212 Third Crater, Moon

Printed in the United States of America.

ISBN: 9798434770132

Chapter One
This Can't be Good

Ordinary is not something I'd ever expected to feel again after that night in Hillcrest Park.

I'd imagine sitting in an office doing computer work isn't the sort of thing many immortals rank high on their bucket lists. However, being swallowed alive by a giant demon tends to shift one's perspective. A little dry tedium is a nice change of pace. I'd have to make an *incredibly* wrong move to light myself on fire doing online background checks.

My life has taken so many crazy turns so far, it's almost difficult for me to believe my present reality. It's not exactly an office job since I own the business and it's only me and Tammy working here. But... the trappings of an office job surround me.

It's easy to daydream about going through the all-too-common routine of the nine-to-five. Had nothing supernatural happened to me, I'd likely find this intolerable. Always did sorta feel annoyed way back when as a HUD agent for ending up there instead of something more adventurous and exciting, like FBI. Not annoyed enough to make a big deal out of it, though. I had Danny and kids to think of. Didn't want to get *too* dangerous.

But an office job? All day every day behind a computer? Bleh. It would've driven me bonkers.

Now? Not so bad.

Will I continue doing this for the next 200 years? Who knows? Probably not. That far in the future, private investigators might be automated, too. Maybe the government will create an AI that monitors everyone all the time.

Okay, if thoughts like this are starting to swirl around, it's probably time for me to go do something in the field and get some air.

I click over to my 'ticket tracking' software app and see what we have in our waiting list. Process serving isn't often exciting, but it's an excuse to go out for a drive. Occasionally, it can be exciting when the person doesn't want to be served. Once I hand them the paperwork, they lose the ability to ignore whatever court proceeding they're caught up in. Some people go to extreme lengths to dodge process servers. I had one guy jump out a third-story window into the water when I showed up at his office. Heh. Poor bastard was so upset when he realized who helped him back onto dry land. To this day, I bet he still wonders how the heck I got there so fast.

And, ugh. We have only one process case in the system and it looks like Tammy already took it.

Explains why she isn't here.

I can't help but get nervous at the idea of her going off on her own to do one of these. Yeah, it can be as simple as a postal carrier handing someone their mail. Alas, few people are happy to see a process server show up. Even if she wasn't trying to give someone documents they likely don't want, this world isn't terribly safe for a young woman to do anything alone, especially Tammy. She's particularly vulnerable now thanks to damned Elizabeth.

No, the bitch didn't do anything new. She's well and truly destroyed.

I mean the telepathy thing. Her power invaded my daughter's mind from a very young age. She could read minds of those around her by age six. Tammy grew up never having to wonder what anyone around her truly thought—she knew. She didn't develop the ability to read people the normal way because it hadn't been necessary. I'm afraid she will miss serious red flags people give off. Most times people quip sarcastically around her, she gets stuck not knowing if they're being sincere or joking.

Hmm. This one doesn't look too bad. Desmond Carter, age forty-one. He's being sued by his ex-wife over unpaid child support. At least, it doesn't seem terribly unusual on the surface until I read a little more into the case file. Seems this guy has refused to pay child support starting about two years ago because he rejects the government's authority to tell him what to do... and the 'ungrateful little bastards' get way too much as it is. Seems like he's also got a restraining order barring him from any contact with his younger sister. No details of why anywhere I can see, though.

Looks like his three kids are 3, 6, and 7 years old.

Wow, this guy sounds like a real peach. No sooner do I look at the file, two things happen roughly at the same time. One: I get an unusual sense that Tammy is unsafe. Two: Tammy walks in the front door of our office. The second one causes the first one to go away. Like, as soon as I see her in front of me, I stop worrying.

She appears fine, but unsettled, her face bearing the sort of expression she might have after some creepy stranger followed her for a few blocks at night.

"Are you okay?" I ask.

Tammy steps in and lets the door swing shut behind her, then rakes her hand up through her thick, black hair before exhaling hard. I can practically feel the nervousness melting off her. "Yeah. Just a little freaked out." She crosses the room to her desk and sits.

"What happened?"

"Nothing." She leans back, putting her feet up crossed. "I chickened out."

I tilt my head at her. "Something had to happen for you to chicken out."

"I got to the address in the file. Walked up, rang the bell"—she pantomimes pushing a doorbell —"and stood there. Like two minutes later, no one's answered, but it feels like I'm being watched. And not 'good watched' either. Just had this feeling like I should get the heck out of there, so I did."

If my daughter happened to be younger, I'd likely keep my worries to myself to avoid frightening her needlessly. Still tempting to do so, but she's eighteen. It's also a good idea to validate her instincts. "Good call. I got a strange sense of foreboding when I looked at the case file."

She gives me side eye. "Why did you look at the case file?"

"Wanted an excuse to go outside for a bit." I shrug. "Only one ticket in the queue, though."

"Psychic hit?" Tammy bites her lip.

My turn to shrug. "Could be. Wasn't too strong. Maybe because you happened to walk in the door right as I started getting the bad vibes."

Tammy fidgets, pulls her feet off the desk, and leans forward in her chair. "I kinda wonder if I might've gotten something, too. Felt like I was in danger. Like… if I kept waiting too much longer, someone was going to attack me."

"Hmm."

"Think I'm psychic, too?" She perks up.

"Who knows?" I scratch my head. "You were the mother of all telepaths for most of your life. Maybe your brain needs the stimulation and could seek it out in unexpected ways."

"Like magnets?"

I blink at her. "Magnets?"

"Yeah." She nods rapidly. "Like, you know how if you keep exposing a piece of ordinary metal to a magnet, it eventually becomes a weak magnet itself?"

"Oh. Yeah, possible I guess. I mean… we don't really understand anything about psychic phenomena."

"Truth." Tammy leans back with a dramatic sigh. "Most people still think it's made-up nonsense."

I laugh. "Most people who claim to be psychics are con artists."

"Yeah."

"Okay." I click the mouse, changing the 'ticket owner' to me. "I'll deal with this one."

Tammy waves at me in an 'all yours' manner and proceeds to dive into background checking on her computer.

Well, no time like the present. May as well go check the place out now. Doubt the guy will expect another attempt to serve him right away. Unfortunately, I can't exactly kick in his door, hold him down, and stuff the papers into his mouth. That would get me in all sorts of legal trouble. Gotta metaphorically ambush him in a public place… or get him to open the door. In theory, I could satisfy the requirements by throwing the paperwork at him and telling him he's been served, even if he doesn't grasp it, it counts.

I jot down the guy's address—an apartment in Buena Park—on a Post-it note, then feel a bit dumb. Pulling it up on Google Maps for an image is all I'd need to teleport there. Then again, that would kinda defeat the purpose of 'getting out.' Going for a drive is the antidote to sitting in the office all day.

My cell phone rings. Since it's right in front of me on the desk, it's easy to see the caller ID pop up: Detective Sherbet. I'd say if he's calling me during normal work hours, it's probably important… but he is a homicide detective. His important calls come in at crazy hours. At this time of day, there's a roughly equal chance it's important, as he might want my opinion on parenting a gay son. As if my adopting Paxton suddenly made me an authority on such things.

"Hey, detective. What's up?" I ask by way of answering.

"Sam…" Sherbet pauses. Traffic in the background tells me he's outside somewhere. His tone of voice is grim, so this has to be a work related call. "Got a crazy one. Mind meeting me at Acacia Park off Newman Street in Buena Park and take a look at something?"

Weird coincidence. I was already about to go to BP. "Sure. Been looking for an excuse to get out of the office all morning. Whatcha got?"

"Dead guy." He pauses, then lowers his voice barely over a whisper. "Drained of blood. Looks like he got into a fight with a weed eater and lost."

"Ugh…" This sounds all too familiar. Though, I've already had my turn being the person found mauled in a park. It's much better to be on the investigating side than the experiencing side. "No problem. I'll be right there."

Tammy glances at me, her raised eyebrows asking what's going on.

"Great. Thanks, Sam." Sherbet exhales in relief.

"Anytime." I hang up, look at my daughter. "Sherbet needs another pair of eyes. They found a body. Sounds like it might be a vampire attack."

"Coyotes," deadpans Tammy. "It's gonna be blamed on coyotes no matter what *really* happened."

I chuckle. "Yeah, probably. Okay, see you in a bit."

Chapter Two
Hollywood Vampire

Of all the places to find a murder victim, this has got to rank in the top five worst.

Acacia Park is basically a grass field with a handful of trees surrounding a playground for small children right next to a school. There's about a baseball field's worth of room between the school and here, so at least it would have been next to impossible for anyone at the school to witness the grim details.

Newman Street is mostly blocked off at the moment due to a large number of police vehicles.

Sherbet meets me at the roadside as I pull up to park. I stare over the Momvan's steering wheel, past a simple brown sign reading 'Rosen / Acacia Park' at a collection of playground equipment, mostly slides and stuff to climb on. The scene—devoid entirely of children and parents—gives me a brief nostalgic flashback to watching Tammy and Anthony play on similar stuff. No obvious signs of anything unusual strike me, which is somewhat of a relief.

I cut the engine and get out.

"Thanks for hurrying over here, Sam," says Sherbet as he approaches.

"No problem. Whatcha got?"

He heads to the left, waving for me to follow him. "A mom called it in about an hour ago. Think the deceased has been there all night, though."

I walk beside him across the grass toward the westernmost edge of the park property where a large group of officers stands near a beige metal electrical box as big as one of those smart cars. A dark plastic tarp covers something on the ground to the right of the metal cabinet.

"A mom… only an hour ago?" I blink.

"Yeah. Couple people and their kids in the park either didn't notice him or mistook the body for a sleeping vagrant." Sherbet stops walking, bows his head. "One little girl thought the 'poor man' might be lonely and hungry, so she walked over to share her apple."

I cringe. "How bad is it?"

"Not pretty, but it's fairly tame compared to some of the poor bastards I've seen in my time." Sherbet resumes walking.

"Kid okay?"

"Yeah." He exhales. "She just thought the man was 'hurt and bleeding' so she ran to get her mother. As far as I know, the kid still thinks all he needs is a big Band-Aid."

I sigh mentally. Poor kid.

The cops and another detective... I want to say his name is Nelson. Grant Nelson, maybe? Haven't talked to him much. He's pretty young for a detective, only like thirty-three or so, I think Sherbet said. Not a bad looking guy. Part Ryan Reynolds, part Tom Hiddleston's Loki. Just made rank a few months ago. Sherbet's getting older, approaching retirement. Guess he's training his replacement whether he wants to or not. At least the process takes a few years. If I know Sherbet, they're going to have to drag him out of the station house on retirement day. He's in no hurry.

Anyway, the police make room for us as we approach. Sherbet crouches by the tarp and peels it back. One new cop who actually looks younger than Anthony stares at me expectantly, as if he's waiting to watch 'the woman' freak out at the sight of a dead body.

Sorry to disappoint ya, kid.

He visibly frowns when I show zero reaction to the sight of a mutilated corpse. My expression has to be about the same as I'd make if I had a cat and he decided to leave a dead mouse on the kitchen floor. Well, okay, there's a whole lot more sympathy for the dead going on in my head compared to what I'd have for a mouse offering, but outwardly, it's game face.

The dead man lays mostly on his side, rolled slightly to the front, facing the power box. He's early thirties, dressed in khaki pants and a peach-hued polo shirt that's been ripped apart via hundreds of small slices. His hair is black, short, and neat. No facial hair. The reason Sherbet called me is as obvious as the two holes in the man's neck and the lack of blood splatter anywhere in sight.

Three feet from the corpse, tucked behind the power cabinet, is a stack of papers, folders, and hardcover books. Call me crazy, but if someone gets pounced by a pack of coyotes and torn up, the dogs aren't going to neatly stack a whole bunch of stuff the victim was carrying prior to the attack nearby.

I'm also not so sure this is the work of an animal... at least the four-legged kind.

Said pile of books tells me who—or what—ever killed this guy, moved him after the fact. I creep around to the head side of the body and take a closer look at the paperwork. The hardcovers are English textbooks for grade school level students. Some of the papers and a manilla folder *do* have blood streaking on them, as well as grass stains.

"The man was carrying this stuff when he was attacked." I point at the pile. "It must have been scattered all over the ground. After, the killer gathered all of these books, papers, and such up and stacked it here, probably to hide it."

Sherbet nods. "Yeah. Was thinking that." He raises an eyebrow, indicating he's waiting for me to address the undead elephant in the room.

Nelson and three of the patrol officers discuss my presence here. I am officially on contract with the Fullerton PD. And yeah, this is a bit far afield for the case to land on Sherbet's desk, but the Buena Park PD is a little backlogged. I think they have some kind of jurisdictional exchange program going on to help ease the workload. That, and Sherbet has a reputation in this part of the state for being good at 'the weird' cases. This reputation is partially thanks to me. No, I don't care he gets most of the credit. Better that way. Last thing I need is to get famous and have people asking why I'm still here and look not-quite-thirty in fifty more years.

I wonder if Gwyneth Paltrow would market undeath as a cure for getting back a pre-baby body.

Nothing quite like becoming an undead vampire, then having a magical explosion change me into something else to get back into fighting weight. It can be yours, too, for the low-low price of your immortal soul. Call now: 1-866-GET-DEAD. Maybe that's the real reason vampires maintain secrecy... they don't want endless lines of desperate people clambering for undead botox. They'd never get a moment's rest.

Sigh.

At least I'm not technically undead anymore. Can't tell you what I am, but it's not that.

Yes, I adore being able to go to the beach again. No, I do not miss having to wear four gallons of sunblock cream every day.

So yeah, dead guy.

"Name's Joseph Keeley," says Sherbet. "He worked at the Mission school right over there."

I glance up at Sherbet briefly before examining the wounds. "Any idea why a teacher would be out here in the wee hours?"

Sherbet flashes a wry smirk. "Their hours are worse than mine."

"Heh."

I really hate to say this, but the slashes all over his face and chest do resemble the aftereffects of vampire claws. The astute observer can tell them apart from something like a mountain lion's claws, mostly due to depth. Cat claws are curved and come to an icepick like point. Vampire claws are basically nail extensions from hell with sharp edges… essentially really tiny daggers that are sharp all around the sides. Of course, they are mystically tough. Fingernails aren't really good weapons after all. They tend to rip out or break. Vamp claw wounds kinda look like someone got attacked by a fistful of scalpel blades. More slicing than ripping. Cat claws leave narrower, deeper wounds. Coyotes, on the other hand, don't have claws, really. The body has no evidence of animal bites except for the one to the neck.

Whoever attacked Joseph Keeley is either a

vampire or they are familiar enough with vampires to make convincing fake claw wounds. Then again, the strikes appear random and frenzied. Whoever did this shredding either wanted to torture this guy or lacked the presence of mind necessary to aim for vital locations. The slashes are all over the place and relatively shallow. I find a few deeper puncture type wounds near the shoulders that make me picture a vampire, claws extended, grabbing on for the bite and using said claws to hold him still.

No vampire I have ever encountered would leave such an obvious 'vampire attack' victim lying out in the open where they'd be found like this. It's almost a scene from a low budget Hollywood movie. The seeming authenticity of the attack is in direct contrast to the carelessness with which the body was left here. Most vampires avoid killing people when feeding.

The fang marks appear realistic enough to legitimately authentic, being as ripped as they are cut. This wasn't a sensual sort of bite on a willing (or unconscious) victim. Bruising and tearing around the puncture wounds tells me this bite occurred in the midst of a desperate struggle. Although, I'm not exactly much of an expert in that regard. I didn't exactly bite people or animals often during my 'undead phase.' In fact, I tried not to think about having fangs at all. Made me feel too monstrous, which is why I had retracted them permanently.

At a rough guess, the number of times I've had

an up-close look at fresh fang wounds could be counted on one hand… and all at least four years ago or longer. However, as best I can recall, the injury looks fairly real. The spacing between the holes suggests the teeth belonged to a relatively small person. Either a woman or a boy on the younger end of teenage. I don't like the idea of a teacher being shredded by one of his students, but the bite mark isn't small enough to be an actual child. No, this is someone only a little smaller than me. Definitely not an adult man. Either a petite adult woman or an early teenage boy.

Ugh.

After I feel there's nothing more to learn from the remains, I move on to examining the ground. The lack of drag marks tells me the killer had the strength to pick up and carry a dead body. Given what I've assumed from the bite mark—woman or teenage boy—it's further evidence a real vampire might have done this. We're fairly strong, after all.

The cops watch me roaming around like a bipedal bloodhound.

It only takes two minutes for my nose to lead me to a tree near a path leading from the sidewalk to the playground. Behind the tree, there's a decorative 'fence' that's only about eight inches tall. Dark brown wood and giant pegs. Oh, wait, it must be like a balance beam for kids to walk on. I can't see how it serves any function as a barrier. Point being, there's blood spatter on it. More on the grass.

"Sherb," I call.

He comes trotting over. "Got something?"

"Yeah. Blood." I point out the spatter. "The attack happened here."

Sherbet crouches to look at the dark stains on the wooden thing.

I meander in an outward spiral, studying the ground. A few areas look to be footprints. It's impossible to tell if the dead man had been running away from his attacker and they caught them at this spot or if he'd been in the park for some reason at two in the morning. Due to it being more reasonable, I'm going to say he probably worked late at the school and left around midnight or so. Maybe they had a function or something. The vampire—or a really good faker—stalked him from the school. Maybe the victim lived nearby and was on his way home. Chase happened, the killer caught up to him here, and… after killing him, carried the body over to the seclusion of a power box.

"It's not much but… theory." I point out the footprints in the grass and share my thinking.

Sherbet nods through my explanation. "Easy enough to check on where he was last night."

"Does he live nearby?" I ask.

"Yeah. Right there on Graham Circle. Poor bastard died about 400 feet from his house."

I shake my head. "They always say people are most likely to die within two miles of home. Any kin?"

"Yeah. Wife. One-year-old son." Sherbet frowns. "She reported him missing this morning."

"Damn." I hang my head.

"What do you think?"

"I think it's tragic."

He nods. "Yeah, but I mean about this being a, you-know-what."

"Oh." I exhale slowly. Still not sure if I *have* to breathe now, but my body wants to do it by itself again, so there's that. Any little slice of normal is welcome, even if it's a useless old habit. "Looks like a short chase happened. Yeah… this guy was probably walking home from the school late at night. Got ambushed."

"Yeah. That tracks." Sherbet sets his hands on his hips. "The bite isn't like yours, though, right? I mean the one that got you, not the ones you used to do."

I subconsciously rub my throat, then speak in a low voice so no one but Sherbet can hear us. "Yeah, a lot cleaner. This guy didn't have his neck ripped open. Just holes. Real vampires can close the bite wound. The vast majority don't kill when they feed because it draws too much attention. And too much attention means…"

Sherbet knows the answer to this one, having been around me for over a decade. "Vampire hunters."

"Right," I say.

"Question. Do the, ah, holes still close if the victim dies?"

I shrug one shoulder. "Can't say. I've never..." Dammit. Wrong. I think I *did* feed-kill one guy in a parking garage once really soon after becoming a vampire but it was... not my choice. I'd been shot a bunch of times and kinda freaked out of my mind. Whatever inner monster is responsible for vampirism took over, and no—not Elizabeth. Something more primal. Considering I didn't consciously do it and don't really remember it too well, I don't consider myself to have killed on purpose.

"Right." He purses his lips. "So, you're saying this *could* be a real problem."

"It's a problem either way, but yeah. If I'm reading your implication correctly, my gut is saying this one's likely to be all types of woo."

He chuckles. Sherbet tends to refer to supernatural things like vampires, werewolves, and psychics as 'woo-woo nonsense.' Or at least, he used to... before being confronted with undeniable proof of it. He still refers to it as 'woo' sometimes, though he no longer means it dismissively. It's just an easier way to refer to a large collection of crazy crap. Sherbet edges closer to me and whispers: "So, what exactly, are we dealing with here?"

"Well... my guess is this is a real vampire attack, most likely someone out of their mind."

"What do you mean?" He cocks an eyebrow. "Isn't 'out of their mind' kinda normal for them?"

I smile. That he used 'them' to refer to vampires

is not lost on me. He's one of an extremely small number of normal people who know intimate details of my existence. Specifically, that I'm 'something else' now and no longer a bloodsucker. Honestly, telling him that eliminated all the discomfort he tried to hide in my presence before, so it proved a win-win decision.

"More so than that." I glance around to ensure we are still speaking privately, then continue. "I don't know all the possible causes, but vampires can be pushed into what's basically a primal, animalistic state where their rational brain goes on vacation. For however long the fit lasts, they're basically velociraptors with better fashion sense—and opposable thumbs."

He chuckles. "Can you give me an idea of what might've set this one off?"

"Well… maybe he or she got so hungry for blood they freaked out."

Sherbet leans away, obviously kidding.

"Relax. I've evolved." I nudge him and wink. "I'm not that kind of vamp anymore. I find intelligence more stimulating now."

"Uh huh." He folds his arms. "That's what they all say."

I roll my eyes at him.

"You are certain the wounds are real?" he asks.

"Clearly. They exist."

He stares at me. "You know what I mean."

I smile. "As certain as I can be without pursuing

a degree in cryptozoological forensics." I tap a finger to my lip. "There's a weird question."

"What?" He tilts his head.

"Would a doctor specializing in woo creatures be considered a doctor or a veterinarian?"

Sherbet sighs at the ground.

We return to the dead guy. I crouch to examine the injuries again, just to be sure. Someone would have had to be intimately familiar with vampires, as well as basically a trained surgeon, to recreate these injuries to this degree of convincing. "Yeah, I think this is real."

"Guess you'd know." He exhales. Then whispers, "You used to do this sort of thing before you got better, right?"

"Not exactly. I *had*—past tense emphasized—sharp teeth, but don't anymore. Hated thinking about them. Tried to forget they existed. Retracted them on a semi-permanent basis. So, no. I never did the sneak up and bite people thing."

He nods.

Grant gives me a weird look. I think he overheard us. And... he's not freaking out. Dammit. I bet Sherbet told him something. Maybe I should've expected that. A vampire immortal working with the cops is going to go through detectives like people go through dogs. Get a new one every twelve-to-sixteen years. Grant might someday be my new contact. Just as long as he can keep his mouth shut, I'm fine with it. Then again, I have to be. Not like I can make him forget.

I explain my opinion on the fang spacing to point at a woman or teen boy as the likely killer.

"Well..." Sherbet sighs. "If this is a real one, there's not too much I'm going to be able to do here. But, I'll keep the case open for now and see what I can find while you handle the woo-woo angle."

"Sounds good."

I'm drawn again to the tree for no particular reason. That usually means psychic stuff is happening, so I don't fight it. Strange urges are nothing new, but this isn't like suddenly wanting to eat pickles when pregnant. Go figure, Allison calls me a psychic vampire because I feed on mental energy. One would assume it natural for a 'psychic vampire' to have psychic abilities, right? Strange that telepathy isn't one of them. Mind reading and talking in people's heads could be so damn handy, but... oh well. If it means Elizabeth is gone for good, I'll deal.

The strange urge leads me back to the tree near the blood marked grass. A bunch of CSI people are photographing the spot now, so I don't intrude too close. A moment after deciding to let my gaze wander wherever whim takes it, I notice a sneaker print in the dirt at the base of the tree. Marks next to it look like a butt-print detailed enough to recognize the indentations formed by jeans with pockets. It's not enough of a butt print for me to get any true notion of size. Still likely a petite woman or a boy around fourteen. Whoever it was, the vampire must have been sitting here for a while, leaning against the tree.

Hunch tells me they didn't plan on attacking Joseph Keeley... the poor guy just happened to walk by at the wrong time. Definitely an ambush. My thoughts go to dark places. A woman might've freaked out from hunger, but if the vampire's a boy? Had he been a former student of this teacher who had some manner of problem with him? Could this attack have been deliberate? Sitting here waiting for him could indicate intent and planning as easily as it might only mean the vampire happened to be here.

Grr.

This might be an isolated attack, a vampire freaking out on a random stranger. It also might be a boy looking for revenge for whatever beef he had with the teacher. Both of those scenarios point at a one-off situation that won't likely repeat. Good there likely won't be another victim. Bad because it makes finding the killer a real chore, like one of those cold cases that sits for forty years. Also, it's not like the legal system is equipped to deal with vampires. Even if we *do* find the killer, if they're a vampire, this one might end up stuck as an unsolvable cold case, anyway.

On the other hand, if this is just a batshit crazy vampire willing to kill anyone they randomly feel makes for a good target, I have a significant problem on my hands.

Might as well get started rattling the trees, so to speak.

And I think it's going to require a little help from an old friend.

Chapter Three
Parasites

It seems I've been a little removed from the vampire scene as of late.

Not going to complain about it, really. For the most part, it isn't anything I miss. Hollywood likes to glamorize vampires and make them out to all be suave rich high-society types with super powers and no cares in the world. Sadly, the older movies came closer to the truth by portraying vampires as monsters. No, not saying they're all hideous creatures or out prowling in the night looking for unsuspecting peasants to maul.

I'm talking about monstrous in a more insidious sense. Take any blood sucking vampire who is a vampire because they wanted to be, and you've got a great chance of finding someone with a laundry list of psychological disorders and quite possibly a distinct lack of humanity… the sort of people who can laugh when they see a pedestrian crushed by a speeding car or find Andrew Dice Clay funny.

Of course, nothing is absolute. There are some relatively stable vampires out there.

Anyway, I'm relieved to be one step removed from that world now. Crazy thing is I can feed on vampires now, too. Mental energy is mental energy, after all. I don't do it though. Too dangerous. If I drain a mortal of too much psychic energy, they simply pass out and take a long nap while their proverbial batteries recharge. Vampires, at least the undead kind, literally cannot sleep at night. If I take too much from one of them, they can't pass out— they go nuts. As soon as I shut off their thinking mind by draining it empty, the monster inside them takes over.

Fortunately, as far as I'm aware, none of the vampires in the area know I've changed or know how much of a potential threat I could be to their illusion of humanity. Hopefully, if any figure it out, they will understand I am not an idiot and wouldn't do anything to create such an obvious spectacle of supernatural events. Vampire hunters would swarm the area. And sure, they probably wouldn't recognize me since I am essentially alive again… but it would get ugly for everyone here: vampires, hunters, and the mortals caught between them.

This is the sort of conversation I slide into soon

after arriving at Fang's blood club in LA.

His place is in Los Feliz, not far from Hollywood. It's enough of a drive from Fullerton that I spared the Momvan and teleported to his office in the back. A gamble, for sure. Who knows what I might've barged in on? Worse is, Fang wouldn't have minded. Then again, for all his eccentricities, he's not into doing freaky things with women. I really do believe his old girlfriend's death was an accident. If it wasn't, he wouldn't be so fastidiously careful about feeding now.

He's always been sort of an esoteric kind of guy, one of those weird kids in high school who liked to read about Alastair Crowley and demonology and ancient history. Back then, I don't think he took any of it seriously. More wanted to be the edgy goth kid. His obsessive fascination with vampires got him into a ton of trouble, though. Like I said, people who want to become vampires have some mental issues. And even if they don't have bad ones, spending long enough as an undead bloodsucker is likely to create some. In some ways, I have to thank Elizabeth for existing. She gave me an adversary and allowed me to feel like I'd been caught in a war for my soul against an enemy.

Back to Fang. He still looks much like he did the last time I saw him—no surprise, as he's a real vampire now. He's rocking a look somewhere between a European playboy and the counterculture kids who wore trench coats to high school. All black, again, that's him. The only article on him not black is a gold vampire fang pendant... with real teeth.

His teeth.

I know, kinda gross. But those two massive canines defined him as a kid—or, rather, he allowed them to. But that's another story for another time.

He sets me up with a real glass of wine—unlike the copious amounts of blood being served to the real vampires in the place—and soon find myself in a conversation about apocalyptic things like vampire hunters forcing a war with the undead so expansive it spills into the general public awareness.

I know, right? No politics. No Kardashian talk. Just straight to Armageddon. Welcome to my life.

Anyway, Fang thinks such a war would herald the end of the world. As far as Armageddon goes, there are generally two kinds of thinking on the subject, or so Fang claims. One group expects humanity to destroy itself with nuclear war. The other group is waiting for the return of some manner of divine being to punch a giant reset button.

Fang's chasing a third scenario no one ever talks about: a war between vampires and mortals. Werewolves would likely be like America in World War II... dragged in unwillingly and ending up tilting the balance.

Our conversation on the theoretical war to end civilization—where vampires, werewolves, and everything else supernatural goes at it completely un-

concerned with the mortal world being crushed under our rampage—pauses when my cell phone
rings.

"Sec." I pull it out and notice Kingsley on the
ID. "Gotta take this."

Fang smiles. "No problem, Moon Dance." He
obligingly wanders away from the bar to check on
patrons. The place *looks* like a normal bar-slash-
night-club, but its true purpose is to provide blood
to vampires in a discreet manner. Mortals show up
here expecting to buy booze—and do—but a fair
number of them spend an hour or so in a back room
donating blood as well.

No, they don't want to, nor do they remember it.

"Hey, big guy. What's up?" I ask into the
phone.

"So, I've been thinking…"

"Oh, no. What blew up?"

"Hah." He exhales. "Nothing. Just thinking I
want to spend a little more time with you than we
have lately."

I smile to myself. The idea of spending a weekend or something at his place, clothing optional, is
sorely tempting. Paxton's not *little.* Both Tammy
and Anthony are old enough and responsible
enough to watch the house. Despite those facts, my
mom-ness is overactive, verging on pathological.
Part of me hesitates, not wanting to leave 'the kids'
alone, but really… my oldest aren't really children
anymore. One could debate if a thirteen-year-old

should be left on their own for a weekend, but Paxton is relatively mature. And Anthony is basically an adult. In a bizarre twist of reality, I think he's a little more mature than Tammy. Generally, the girls get there first. Of course, Anthony is on a trajectory to becoming an angel, so he might be the exception.

Still, boys do dumb things—like that time Mary Lou's sons decided to play 'World Wrestling' in the backyard and both of them ended up needing casts. They still haven't replaced the picnic table, and it's been almost eight years.

"Sounds lovely," I say.

"Excellent." Kingsley's smile is evident in his tone. "How's Friday night sound?"

"It's only Tuesday."

He pauses. "What does that have to do with anything?"

I fake a whine like an impatient kid. "You're going to make this entire week feel like it's taking forever."

"I could shuffle things around and pick you up tonight?"

"Ooh, tempting." I bite my lip. "It's a bit late to go out, and we already had dinner. No, Friday is fine. I'd rather have the whole weekend free after. Kinda got a case from Sherbet, but it's one of *those* situations."

"Those situations?"

I picture him raising an eyebrow and making that face he always makes that looks like a confused dog, head slightly tilted. The mental image makes me want to wrap my arms around him right now. "I'm expecting to look into it for a couple of days, get nowhere, and the suspect vanishes into the nothing from whence they came. Sherbet found a body. Looks like a vampire attack. I'm inclined to think it's a one-off. Still kinda early to tell exactly what's going on. Just started today."

"Ahh. Okay. Let me know if you need my help with anything."

"Thanks. I will."

We exchange slightly mushy goodbye-for-nows and hang up.

As if he'd been watching me out of the corner of his eye, Fang heads back over as soon as I put the phone away. He's giving me this dangerous look… a 'good dangerous' like he'd totally do things with me we shouldn't be doing while I am in a committed relationship with Kingsley. It's a somewhat awkward relationship we have. He's a good friend, and yes, he is sincerely a friend… but he really wants it to be more than simple friends. Flattering, honestly. Considering some of the women he gets in this place, I'm hardly the prettiest. We *are* really close to Hollywood and his club is developing a reputation among the elites. Rumor has it, drinks named after celebrities are—when ordered by a vampire—the blood of the actual person who came here and 'donated'. (If a mortal orders one, they get some crazy mixed alcohol drink.) The celebrity blood is really expensive though, something like five to ten grand a feeding or even more depending on who it came from.

No, it serves no special purpose other than letting some vampire feel artificially special for having 'dined on' someone rare and exclusive. It's as stupid as a mortal paying $2,500 for a steak dinner when they could have gone to TGIF's.

Even if I still needed blood, that's a hard pass from me. Sure, I've fantasized about doing things to Tom Hiddleston, but... this is a bit too creepy for me. Drinking human blood *always* bothered me, but taking it from an unwilling person who didn't even know they were mesmerized and drained a bit? Ugh. So wrong. Yes, I resist the urge to look at a menu to see if he's even on it. Probably not. Isn't he English? This place is kind of a long ride for him.

Anyway.

Fang leans on the bar nearby, still gazing at me in a 'I really wish we could be together' sort of way. "It is wonderful to see you again in person rather than chat."

"Yeah. Sorry. Things have been crazy."

Fang knows about my change; that is, from bloodsucking fiend to energy-sucking not-quite-a-fiend. Some might think it's foolish of me to still trust him, but I do. We've shared things with each other we can't tell anyone else. Hate to say it, but there's some stuff he knows that I haven't even told Kingsley, and it's not a trust issue there. What does a werewolf know about the inner workings of undead vampire struggles?

"I get it." He smiles again, showing off his fangs. I should say, his 'new' fangs. The canine teeth he was born with got pulled out. Bastards. When he became a *real* vampire, the Universe repaired him. "I also get you're here for a reason more than hanging out. What's a woman with kids doing at a bar at this hour?"

I laugh. "You're good at reading people. You should've been a detective."

For a few seconds, his 'cool' persona crumbles entirely to genuine laughter. The notion of *him* being a police detective is so patently ludicrous it breaches his defenses.

"So, there's a body…" I explain the situation with the dead teacher. "Wondering if you might have heard anything about new vampires in the area." The question's out of my mouth before I realize the Void is gone and the dark masters scattered to the four winds.

"Why are you hesitating?" He gestures at me, seeming amused. "Say too much to a non-cop?"

"No. Not that." I furrow my brows. "Is it still even possible to make new vampires, given the dark master situation?"

Fang nods. "Oh, surely."

"You sound confident there. Been studying ancient Sumerian blood magic or something?"

"Yes, but that has nothing to do with it." He sips

from his dark red cup.

Okay, I can't tell if he's joking or serious. Fang has the same grin on his face when he's being serious as he does when he's pulling my leg. At the moment he's kinda channeling some kind of meta thing where Christian Bale is playing Jared Leto playing the Joker. At least, that's my impression of what's going on with his facial features.

"Dark masters weren't necessary for the creation of vampires… or werewolves… or anything else." Fang waves dismissively. "They're rather akin to parasites, hitchhiking on the process as a way out of where they'd been stuck. Vampires existed long before those ancient mystics tried to make themselves immortal."

I blink, taking a moment to process this thought. No one, as far as I know, is sure exactly how long vampires have existed. While the notion of a Neanderthal vampire is kinda silly to me, magic *is* part of the world. So… who knows?

"What would the differences be?" I ask.

He shrugs. "Not sure entirely… beyond they wouldn't have a voice in the back of their head. I assume the natural ones would be somewhat darker in temperament. They'd likely be unable to withstand the sunlight at all. While they can be wholly irritating, the dark masters did offer something of a symbiotic benefit. It's also possible they might not be able to tolerate animal blood. But…" Fang waves his hand around randomly. "This is me theorizing. The differences might not even be noticeable. It's not as though I've met one yet in person and been aware of it."

"Right." I half-sit on a barstool. Yes, I'm the idiot in an expensive vampire bar sipping an alcoholic drink instead of blood. No one would know from looking at my glass, though. Purely trying to act natural. "So, if it's possible new vampires can be made despite the sparsity of dark masters—"

"They aren't gone. Just, scattered." Fang holds up a finger. "Dark masters do still exist and might still decide to insert themselves into the process, but I am sure they aren't *required*."

"So, have you heard any rumors about a new one around here? Specifically, Buena Park."

He shakes his head. "No. I have not."

I shift my jaw side to side, thinking. "One of these masterless vampires... would they be prone to killing when they feed?"

Fang gazes at the ceiling in contemplation for a moment. Ever talk comic books with a nerd? Discussing vampires with Fang is about the same as getting into a conversation about who'd win in a fight between Hulk and Thor with a forty-two-year-old guy who owns a comic book shop, has 40,000 issues of various comics in arm's reach, and Wolverine bed sheets at home.

"This is me theorizing again." Fang smiles. "My guess is they would likely have less of a problem morally with the act of killing. The older, more traditional vampires are, I think, a bit closer to what you'd call evil. However, for the sake of self-preservation, they wouldn't want to draw attention to themselves. Perhaps you've encountered the work of a Nathrezein?"

"Gesundheit."

He chuckles.

"Wanna try that again? What on Earth is a Nathra-whatever?"

"Nathrezein," says Fang while holding his hands up like that wild-haired 'It Was Aliens' guy on all those memes. Uh oh. I got Fang going. "Remember our discussion about souls?"

"Which one?"

"Hah. Fair point." Fang winks. "Okay, you know how immortals like us have our souls detached from the creator and fully contained within our bodies."

"Right. The 'no reincarnation' thing."

"Exactly." He laces his fingers together. "A Nathrezein is a vampire that went in the other direction. The soul detached from the body and went back into the primordial soup. Something *else* takes over the body."

"Oblivion?"

"No, it's basically just death. The poor bastard whose body got stolen gets to reincarnate. They're not in there anymore. Dark energies have hijacked the flesh. It's not the same person inside."

"Why have I never heard of these before?" I

raise an eyebrow.

Fang puts a chummy arm around my shoulders, wags his eyebrows, and mutters, "Most likely because you are not a vampire hunter."

"Right." I smirk.

He lets go, leans on the bar. "Nathrezein don't usually show up in the States. They exist primarily in the Middle East, Asia, and parts of Siberia. They're also pretty short lived as vampires go. If one lasts fifty years, it's an achievement."

"Ticking clock?" I ask.

"No. They're monstrous and not at all subtle. Usually end up being hunted down."

"Oh." I shift my weight on the stool. Time to let the other cheek do some work. Yeah, I could properly sit on it, too, I suppose. "What are the odds one of them made it to California?"

"Just holes on the neck? Not torn out?"

"Holes. Mild tearing. Frenetic, random claw marks all over the face, shoulders, and chest."

Fang nods. "You're not looking at one of those Nathrezein, then. My guess is a new vampire who lost control. Probably didn't realize what they'd become or that they needed blood. Got a whiff of the dead guy and… well… like a double chocolate cake sitting outside an over-eaters anonymous meeting."

"Right…"

He edges a little closer, but it's not creepy or even unpleasant. He's one of those people who thrives on social connections, likes being close to others. We're not touching… yet, but our bodies are much closer than most people would find comfortable for a conversation with someone they aren't dating.

"It's pretty rare for us to kill when feeding nowadays," says Fang. Of course, he knows I know this. He's talking to talk, to prolong our time. "It's the main reason we've gone from 'monsters' to being considered 'cool.' Back in Dracula's day, vampires preyed on peasants and left bodies littered around like beer cans. People feared and despised us."

"Yeah." I sip my drink.

"Some genius about 300 years ago decides, 'hey, we only need blood. No point to kill anyone because it only gets the mortals pissed off.' So… we turned ourselves into giant mosquitoes."

If he'd have said that two seconds sooner, I'd be choking on my drink. When I manage to get my laughter under control, I just shake my head at him.

He holds his arms out to either side. "Hey, it worked, didn't it? People either don't believe we are real or they think vampires are cool."

"True. Can't argue that."

Fang picks his blood drink off the bar again and chugs the last mouthful. He's one of the rare guys who can 'chug' a drink and look smooth doing it, not like a beered-up frat boy. "I'll do some asking around, see if anyone's aware of new blood in the area. Newbies don't usually stay hidden too long, especially if they're clueless and careless."

"Great. Thanks."

"So, uhh…" He gives me a light elbow nudge. "When are you going to stop messing around with that giant furball and get serious with me?"

In most cases, someone saying that so bluntly would make me angry. But… it's Fang. His expression and tone of voice are not serious. This is a joke he hopes might come true. He isn't earnestly trying to talk me into leaving Kingsley.

"You know I love Kingsley and there's no chance of me leaving him."

Fang holds up a finger. "Unless you catch him cheating again."

I frown. "He won't."

"But if he does?"

"Ugh." I pinch the bridge of my nose. "Please don't make me think about that."

He raises both hands. "Hey, sorry. I won't. No need to rush. He's a werewolf. I'll just wait it out. The two of us have all the time in the universe."

I narrow my eyes. "You're not exactly endearing yourself to me right now with that line of logic."

Fang bares his teeth in a rogue's grin. "You know you love me."

I roll my eyes, but he is kinda irresistible in an annoying older brother sort of way. I hug him. "Yeah. I do love you, but not the way you're hoping for."

"At least not yet."

"Ever the optimist." My turn to wink. "I should get going."

"All right. Please don't be a stranger, Moon Dance."

I hug him one more time. "I won't. And thank you for helping out."

"Anything you need, I'm happy to oblige." Fang seems reluctant to let go of my hand, but lets my fingers slip away.

Damn. How can a guy suggest I leave the man I love for him and I end up still feeling bad for him? As crude as his comment was... he's not wrong. Werewolves don't live forever, just a few thousand years or so. Fang and I, well... we can be killed, but time alone won't do it. He's got the vampire thing down pat, for sure. He's completely patient enough to wait for the sands of time.

I hope he at least has the decorum to wait for me to finish mourning Kingsley when the day comes. Of course, there's a lot of guesswork there. Something might destroy me or Fang well before Kingsley runs out of time. Not to mention, something might destroy Kingsley before he dies naturally.

Only thing I can really do is try to make the most out of the here and now.

And on that note, I'm going home to my kids.

Chapter Four
Milo

One moment, I'm in a club full of vampires. The next, I'm racing around my kitchen trying to get three teenagers ready for school.

Not literally a minute; it only feels like it. I slept pretty hard. One of those 'as soon as my head hit the pillow I was out' nights, which morphed directly into the morning chaos. Is it strange that even with my modestly accelerated reflexes, it's a struggle to keep up? Make coffee, get breakfast ready— yeah, that's on me. I like to do real breakfast instead of just letting the kids forage on their own.

At least we're well past the point of me needing to pick outfits and get the kids into their clothes. That part, they can handle on their own now— mostly. Paxton takes the longest to get ready because she has trouble deciding on her outfit. She'll put something on, start to leave her room and go back to change because the outfit suddenly 'doesn't work.' Got lucky with the other two. Neither of them cared at all about fashion. To a point. Tammy would only wear black or grey for a couple of years, but she's emerged from the other end of that phase.

The three of them are in wildly different moods. Tammy's in this 'ugh, get it over with already' attitude toward school. This is her last year of high school and she's just 'so done' with it all. Without her telepathy, she's uncomfortable around people since she can't tell what they're thinking and struggles to interpret body language cues. Poor kid is too ready to enter the adult world without realizing what she's leaving behind. Alas, nature works that way. She hasn't said much about college or art school or anything lately.

The mom in me is simultaneously proud of her for working at my PI office and dreading the idea she'll end up with only a high school education working middling to low end jobs for the rest of her life. She's definitely on a different wavelength than most. The whole nine-to-five career thing, to her, is an unnatural perversion of the way nature intended us to live. Gah, she's starting to sound like my parents. That said, she doesn't seem to mind the hours at Moon Investigations... and even seems to enjoy it. Worse, has a natural knack for it.

Right. Uh oh.

On the other end, is Paxton. She's got so much happy energy in the morning. Girl can't wait to get to school and see her friends. Her contagious enthusiasm propels her around the kitchen with the freneticism of a human-sized faerie who happens not to have wings. The contrast from her makes Tammy seem downright moody even though she, like me, is in the 'I haven't had a full cup of coffee yet, do not speak to me' doldrum.

In the middle, is Anthony. He's neither excited nor glum about school or his upcoming day. Kid takes everything in stride. Can't really say it's a remarkably strong-willed personality or overdeveloped maturity. He's on a path to immortality, I think, and has a heck of a future in wait for him. I think he's merely savoring the time he gets to be with his family.

He's also back in normal high school. Not gonna lie, I prefer having him home rather than away at Max's boarding school. Whatever course fate has charted for my son is not one that relies on whatever he'd learn there. We're both fairly sure he's going to end up becoming a literal angel at some point. My guess is the job comes with a proprietary user's manual as well as on the job training mortals simply can't provide.

Neither he nor I know exactly when he'll transform, evolve, or whatever you want to call it. He believes it won't happen until after Tammy dies— hopefully of old age. One of the big reasons he gave for wanting to come home and go back to his old school was to be around to protect his sister. Or should I say sister*s*, plural.

After the kids pile into Tammy's Prius and head off for school, I stand there in the doorway staring at the little blue car getting smaller. Immortality has a flaw. I'm going to watch my kids grow old and die. I'm going to watch the same thing happen to Mary Lou. I'd say the same about my brothers, but I haven't seen any of them since they left home at eighteen. We're not exactly close. No bad blood, just... going in different directions. It would upset me to think about them growing old if I saw them more often. Maybe it should upset me and I'm flawed for not being as upset.

Is it bad that I'm not terribly worried about my parents' inevitable death?

The older I get—or should I say, the more time that passes—the more I resent them for the childhood they gave us. It's definitely not hate, but... let's just say I won't exactly cry at their funeral—if I even go. Already, I look too young to be Samantha Moon. Not sure if they have any friends or relatives who'd show up, but if so, none of them would believe I am who I say I am. Mary Lou looks older now than my memory of Mom. The last time I saw my mother face-to-face, I was still mortal. If 'Samantha Moon' shows up at any sort of family event, they're going to expect a woman who looks significantly older than I do.

Bleh. I don't know how to handle that, so I'm going to stop thinking about it.

I turn to face the interior of the living room. How can a house be so dear and so painful at the same time? I can't look at anything here without a flood of memories of my kids being small, of Danny before he descended into madness and became a complete ass, of the life we might have had without the supernatural weirdness thrusting itself upon us. Would Danny have turned into a selfish, controlling, creep if I hadn't become a vampire?

Meh. These what-if questions are more pointless than braille on the keys of a drive-through ATM.

I sit on the couch for a while, slowly enjoying my coffee. Yes, I'm an addict. When I head out to my office in a few minutes, I'll be stopping by Starbucks for yet another coffee—and some mental energy. Think I've developed an association between that place and feeding. The sight of those green signs makes me hungry now. Some might consider it cruel to drain mental energy from a bunch of people on their way to work in the morning craving a caffeine pick up. Perhaps my siphoning off a little bit from everyone around me results in a few of them crashing hard at like two in the afternoon when the coffee high wears off.

Dunno.

On particularly slow days at HUD, I nearly napped at my desk once or twice in the afternoon. It's a normal part of working an office job. And speaking of office jobs… I should get going.

***

The security company who contracted me for background checks just hired a new wave of guards.

Okay, wow. Gotta run backgrounds on forty candidates. This deal is good for me as it's a steady source of income. Security guards have a high attrition rate. The hours suck, the work is boring as hell, and not many people can handle it for extended periods of time. Some people don't mind it and work their entire careers in security. Good for them. I'd never be able to do that. Sitting around a mostly empty place at night just existing there in case something happens? Ugh. My brain would melt out of my ears from the boredom.

I'd say I'm shocked at some of the things I find in the background searches, but I'm not really. People can be dumb. Why would someone who's been arrested fourteen times for possession of narcotics bother applying for a security job? Got me. Maybe they're hoping the place skimps on background checking. Maybe they think the place won't care.

An hour and thirty-seven minutes into my day at work, the phone rings.

I answer. "Moon Investigations." Yes, I shortened it from Moon Investigative Services... at least when I answer the phone. What can I say? I like things short and sweet.

"Hello," says a woman who sounds worried and frantic. "Are you a private investigator?"

Yeah, she's clearly upset. Who calls a PI and asks if they're a PI? "Yes. I am. How can I help you?"

"My son Milo is missing. The police haven't been able to find anything." She pauses, taking a few deep breaths, I assume, to hold back an emotional outburst. "My husband and I want to hire someone to help find him. One of the cops gave us your name."

Dammit. Missing kid cases always tear me up inside with worry. I can't say no, because then if I do, I'll never know how it turns out and spend the next several decades wondering if the boy ever turned up alive. If I accept the case, I'm going to be a ball of anxiety until I find the kid.

"I'd love to help. How old is Milo?"

"He turned thirteen a few weeks ago," says the woman.

Oh shit. Dammit brain. You would go there. As soon as she says 'thirteen,' I'm instantly picturing the bite mark on the dead teacher. Some boys that age are bigger than others, though. There are a few kids in Anthony's class who—despite being sixteen and seventeen—could pass for twelve. Conversely, other boys who *are* twelve look more like seventeen. So, I shouldn't jump to conclusions so fast. Missing boy about the right age to be of size to make that bite mark doesn't prove anything. Coincidence is a thing, after all. Still, it's something to keep at the back of my mind.

"Has he been acting in any way strange or unusual prior to when he disappeared?" I ask, hoping *not* to hear her say he was often sleepy, couldn't get out of bed, and shied away from sunlight.

"No," says the woman. "Not that I noticed. Everything seemed just fine. Well... I mean, fine, all things considered."

Uh oh. "What things?"

She sighs. "He's been a little quiet and distant lately. I think it's because we just moved to this area from Ohio. He misses his friends. My husband thinks he might've run away and tried to get on a bus or train to go back to Maysville."

"That's a hike for a kid his age. Did he seem so upset with the move to take such an extreme step?"

"Not really, but I don't know." The woman pauses to collect herself. "I'm so worried sick right now, it's not easy for me to think straight about anything. Maybe he was, and I just didn't notice. Prior to his disappearance, I had been trying to tell myself everything would be okay. He'd make new friends and be happy."

I jot down some notes and go through some basic questions. Her name is Kaitlyn Boone, husband Ben. They have a daughter who's younger, only nine, named Saffron. Pretty name. They recently inherited Kaitlyn's parents' house on West Las Palmas Drive in Fullerton. Fairly close. Nice, large house. She rambles a bit about how they're going to try to make a go of it in California, but if it doesn't work out, they'll sell the place and move back to Ohio. They had been living in an apartment in Ohio, but Ben's parents still live there, so they'd have help if they need to go back. It's obvious to me she's rambling about this and that to keep her mind off Milo's possible fate. But I can't let her talk in circles forever.

"Why don't I stop by and have a look around? I'll need to learn as much as I can about Milo."

"All right." Kaitlyn draws in a breath. "Are you planning to stop by soon?"

"How about right away?"

"Great. We'll be here. And thank you." Kaitlyn exhales hard. "I... the police aren't saying much. They think he might've run off, too."

"Okay. I'm out the door as soon as we get off the phone."

"Thanks. See you soon."

We hang up.

I stand there for a moment staring at the address on the Post-It note. Dammit. Just what I needed on top of a vampire killer... a missing kid.

Grr. I *really* hope these cases aren't as connected as I'm afraid they are.

Chapter Five
Eerie

The Boones don't live too far from me.

It's a slightly longer trip from my office to their house than if I'd been at home. I pass a number of huge houses—compared to mine—before locating the address Kaitlyn gave me. It's no mansion, but it's easily three times the size of my house. I'm not jealous, honest. More space means more work to keep it clean, more mortgage, more taxes.

Maybe it borders on unhealthy, but I really do love my little house. In fact, despite my status as an immortal, my possessiveness toward my house might be so strong it overpowers the natural processes of the universe to result in me haunting the place when something finally destroys me.

I'm too focused on the idea of a missing kid to

spend any more than two seconds taking in the size of the home. It's relevant to the upcoming investigation. Everything I can learn or infer about the family helps me figure things out. Kids in somewhat more well-to-do families have a higher likelihood of 'running away' over stupid crap, like having their cell phone taken away as punishment or being told they can't go to a party on a school night. Not saying every family that's financially comfortable raises entitled brats, merely the odds of this turning out to be a minor issue are there.

Of course, rich kids running away over cell phone privileges don't usually go too far. Friend's house maybe. Or they spend one night in random places, get a taste of reality, and run home—provided no one hurts them first. Kaitlyn mentioned they'd recently moved from Ohio. Cross-country moves can be rough on kids. Uprooting them from their friends and familiar surroundings isn't easy.

Wait... she said they inherited the house. Maybe they aren't quite as well off as the size of the property would imply. Even without a mortgage to pay, the property taxes on a place this big would be kinda brutal around here. I'm sure they can handle it or they would've simply sold the house immediately without moving into it. So, yeah. They used to live in an apartment in Ohio. Good chance I'm not dealing with a kid who has an entitled attitude. Which means...

He could be on a bus right now heading 'home.'

A soft *whud* from the Momvan's door closing behind me strikes me as unusually loud. Before I can fully process the oddity of it, my attention goes to the house, drawn by a pronounced sense of unease. Seems I'm having a run on eerie houses lately. Hopefully, little Milo wasn't abducted by a weird cult worshiping octopus-faced monsters. To be fair, the energy wafting from this house is significantly less powerful. It's the kind of psychic impression mediums probably get from a property where a murder happened, or so I assume. If I count as a 'medium' now, I'm still kinda new at it. Next time I go to a house where someone was killed, I'll take notes.

But, yeah. There is definitely something unusual going on here. Not to sound too horror movie cliché here, but it almost feels like the house is watching me.

The presence of one marked police car and an ever-so-obvious unmarked car tells me there's likely a detective or two here. I never understood why police departments use certain models of cars for their unmarked. Like Crown Vics are so damn obvious police cars pretending not to be, they might as well just throw light bars on them and paint them black and white.

Feeling something like a beetle approaching a cat likely to eat it, I walk up the long path connecting the sidewalk to the porch. Voices, mostly male, murmur within. Sounds like a detective is speaking to the father about Milo's habits, behaviors, any new friends he's made around here, and whatever routine he might have established.

When I ring the bell, the conversation stops. The eeriness remains.

A moment later, a late-thirties blonde woman answers the door. She kinda reminds me a bit of the *I Dream of Genie* actress… if she hadn't slept in three days. An oversized grey Ohio State sweatshirt speckled with coffee stains tells me that, yeah, she really hasn't slept in a few days. Along with the opening door, a wave of energy rolls over me like hot air blowing out from an overheated room. It's not actually heat, though. It passes in a second and is gone. The air in front of me isn't noticeably different in temperature from the outside. Maybe a ghost just ran me over.

Unfortunately—scratch that, *fortunately*—I can't see them anymore. Going from blood vamp to energy vamp, and possessed to unpossessed… yeah, I've gone through some changes.

"Mrs. Boone?" I ask.

She opens her mouth, seemingly not sure what to say. I don't believe I look like a Jehova Witness, a pollster, or a sales weasel… she clearly doesn't realize who I am.

"Samantha Moon." I offer a hand. "We spoke on the phone not too long ago."

"Oh!" She bites her lip. "You got here so fast. I didn't…"

"I'm local." My smile appears to reassure her somewhat.

She takes a step back and beckons me in. "Sorry. The police are still here."

"That's fine." I enter the foyer and glance around, searching for the source of the *weird*. Thankfully, the walls aren't moving, the chairs aren't breathing on their own, and no creepy humanlike faces peer at me from dark places. The interior *looks* perfectly normal in every way... it simply doesn't feel it.

The living room is huge and overwhelmingly beige. Three men stand in a triangle between a sectional and a modestly sized television. I'm sure it's actually huge, but the room is so big it makes the screen appear small. One's a uniformed cop. The other is, I'm guessing, a detective based on the gun holster straining to stay wrapped around a muscular chest. His white polo shirt looks more painted on than worn. Man number three must be Ben Boone, the father. Poor guy looks broken with worry. He's still wearing plaid pajamas and has a not-quite-here expression. In contrast to his zoned out face, his responses to the detective are coherent. My guess is fatigue from lack of sleep plus worry plus the denial of 'this isn't happening to us'.

After I briefly explain to Detective McMahan who I am, I follow Kaitlyn to the kitchen. It's a habit of mine to always mention I'm a former fed when talking to the cops. They tend to roll their eyes at PIs otherwise. I need them to be as open and helpful as possible, not ignoring me as some useless idiot trying to cosplay as a detective.

A little girl with blonde hair and hazel eyes watches me from the archway separating the kitchen from the dining room. Two tiny pink fuzzy bunny faces peek out at me from the hem of her nightgown—slippers. This must be Saffron, the daughter. Surprisingly, for a nine-year-old, she appears emotionally collected, but gives me this pleading 'you're gonna find Milo, right?' stare that makes it difficult to look at her without having a lump form in my throat.

"Coffee?" asks Kaitlyn while gesturing at a pot already made.

I don't like to impose, but my read on her says it will calm her down if I accept... so I do.

"Mom won't let me have coffee," mutters the girl. "I'm too young."

"A bit, yes." I smile at her. Neither of them need to know I let Tammy have coffee at age eleven. She drank it without asking permission as a form of rebellion. Like, some kids smoke pot or drink alcohol. She thought slurping down coffee was going to 'get us back' for the problems. Us being Danny and I. I pretended to be a little upset, so she didn't do anything more extreme, but if coffee is the hardest drug she hits, I'm a happy mom.

Keeping one ear and a quarter of my brain on the conversation between Ben and the detective, I engage in fairly casual conversation with Kaitlyn, trying to establish an understanding of Milo. She's got several printed photos—from his school—ready. The boy is also blond like his sister. While it's not too easy to get a sense from a portrait, he seems a little small for his age but highly photogenic. He and his sister could be catalog models for Macy's or some such thing.

In this particular photo, taken soon before they left Ohio, he's smiling and looks completely normal. According to his mother, he didn't really want to move and kept trying to talk them out of it. However, when they ultimately did go through with relocating to California, he stopped complaining and became quiet. When engaged with some activity, he seemed normal. When idle, he'd get morose and just sit there looking sad.

Granted, it's only been a month since they moved. If he misses his friends, some degree of coping is to be expected.

Saffron admits to crying a bit over being far away from her best friends, too, but she's mostly dealt with it. The kid tells me she and her friends still talk all the time. She also lets fly a zinger when she says she expects her parents will run out of money soon, have to sell the house, and they'll be back in Ohio.

How true that is, I don't know. Still, gotta be rough as parents to get a break like a free house only to have both your kids hating the change. If I had to guess, I'd say Saffron's probably going to manage staying here just fine, even if she's being a little bit of a drama queen right now.

As for Milo… it's hard to say. I've got to take his mother's mental state into account. She, of course, is upset, worried, and likely guilty over his disappearance. Consequently, she may overstate the negative behaviors she observed in her son.

The conversation with the detective sounds fairly normal. He's going through the usual checkboxes: friends, hangouts, habits, and so forth. With the family being in the area for such a brief time, Milo hasn't had the chance to make close friends yet. His father can't think of anywhere he might have gone to hide out beyond potentially trying to go back to Ohio. Ben—the father—doesn't think his son would run away for two reasons. One: Milo wouldn't want to hurt his parents and scare them like that. Two: the boy's not the adventurous type. Dad thinks he'd be too frightened to risk a solo cross-country trip.

I start asking Kaitlyn about her son's hobbies and after-school activities. She confirms he isn't into sports. Most of his free time is spent either drawing, messing around with his guitar, or playing video games. Neither he nor his three friends back in Ohio had much love for the outdoors.

"I know Ben isn't open to the idea…" Kaitlyn sighs. "But… I really think Milo is on his way back to Ohio."

Saffron responds with a faint 'no' headshake, her mother doesn't notice.

"Don't think so?" I ask, raising an eyebrow at the girl.

"No. Milo's too chicken." Saffron puffs a strand of hair out of her eyes. "And he would'a told me he was going home, so I didn't get sad."

Kaitlyn refills her coffee. "Maybe he didn't tell you because he didn't want you telling me or your father?"

"No. He wouldn't worry about that." Saffron folds her arms on the table, then puts her head down.

"You would have told us?" Kaitlyn turns to look at her.

"I decline to answer on grounds of self-intimi-nation," mumbles Saffron.

"Incrimination?" I suggest, trying not to smile.

"Yeah, that." The girl waves at me. "What she said."

Kaitlyn stares helplessly at me.

"Can you think of anything Milo might have done differently in the last week or so? Like sleeping in late?" Yes, it's my thinly veiled attempt to confirm he's not the new vampire in town.

"He stayed in his room a lot." Saffron swishes her bunny slippers back and forth. "He didn't want to PlayStation with me anymore. Like we *always* do two-player games."

"It's their thing." Kaitlyn flicks her thumbnail at

58

the mug in her hands. "They sometimes yell at each other but it's like… in fun."

Saffron lifts her head off her arms, a curtain of blonde mostly hiding her face. "We only yell at each other in the competition games. But we're not really mad at each other."

Hmm. Kid sulking in his room could be a side effect of moving, but it could also be due to the sluggishness of post-vampiric conversion. That weird supernatural energy in the air here could be from the presence of a vampire in the house. No one else other than me appears to even notice it. Even Saffron is seemingly oblivious to it, and children are often the first to respond to negative supernatural energy. If a kid shows signs of being randomly afraid of a place for no good reason, chances are high they're picking up on something adults can't detect.

The detective and cop leave, promising to do all they can on their end, and that they will be in touch as soon as they know more.

After a moment, perhaps to gather himself, Ben joins us in the kitchen, where we continue talking about the situation. The more I get from the parents describing their son in relatively normal terms given the circumstances of their relocation, the more I set aside the notion of Milo running away. This kid just doesn't sound like he's got the personality to rebel so much. He also wouldn't want to be separated from his family. They seem quite close.

"Would you mind if I looked around his bedroom?" I ask.

"Uhh." Ben glances at his wife, then back at me. Shrugs. "I guess. Don't see how it would hurt, really."

"Sure." Kaitlyn nods.

"I'll show you." Saffron bolts from her chair and scampers out of the kitchen.

I follow the child through the dining room to a hallway. She hangs a hard right before going into the living room and goes down a hall. Milo's room is almost at the end on the right. An explosion of girly stuff on the door next to his identifies it as Saffron's room. Milo's door is plain.

Inside, it superficially resembles the bedroom of an adolescent boy. Several cardboard boxes sit on the rug on the right, likely containing the posters, model planes and cars, or other decorations he hasn't gotten around to putting up yet. My first focus is the windows. The shades are down, but it may or may not represent an attempt to hide from sunlight. Can't say it's an extreme effort to block out sun. Taking it as a sign he spent the past week gradually turning into a vampire with a sunlight aversion is a bit of a jump. Maybe the sun hit him in the eyes while he lay in bed.

"I think he's kinda hoping we change our minds," says Ben, behind me.

I look at him. "Hmm?"

Ben points at the boxes. "He hasn't unpacked

some of his things. Room still looks like we just got here."

"Nah, he's just laaaazy," says Saffron.

Or sad. Ben could be right. Kid's trying to save the work of packing it all up again if they end up moving. But… even in a worst-case situation, they wouldn't be out the door *that* fast. I meander around the room, tracing my fingers over various surfaces. Yeah, I'm hoping to pick up something on a psychic level. Hopefully, touching stuff doesn't make me seem like a weirdo.

The odd vibe of the place is in here, too. Can't say it's any stronger or weaker. His closet doesn't show any signs of a hasty packing job suggesting a deliberate running away.

"Does he have a backpack?" I ask.

Ben nods, then points at it on the floor by the dresser. "Still here. If he did run away, he didn't put much planning into it."

"Dad…" Saffron leans against him. "Milo didn't run away. I heard him yell."

Ben's expression goes frustrated. "Ms. Moon, she's got an imagination. We were all home at the time. Even if, for some reason, Milo went out to the yard, Kait and I would have heard the yell, too. I don't understand how only Saf could have heard Milo cry out."

The girl flaps her arms in a 'how should I know?' manner.

"Humor me," I say to Ben before making eye

contact with the daughter. "What did the yell sound like? Scared?"

She scrunches her nose. "No, not really. Like, if you went to go down some stairs but fell... that kinda scream. But more 'boy.'"

"More boy?" I ask.

Saffron nods. "Yeah, he didn't scream like..." She shrieks like a little girl having a frog stuffed down the back of her dress.

Ben cringes.

"He yelled more like..." Saffron belts out a yell that's essentially a child's g-rated version of 'holy shit.'

I picture a boy walking on a brick wall or something and it breaks out from under him. So... it's a sound of surprise with fear. It does not seem like the sort of cry a thirteen-year-old boy would give if a strange person tried to abduct him into a van. Considering there is no broken playground equipment in their backyard, I'm tempted to say the yelp might have been caused by suddenly discovering vampire fangs—or noticing he no longer had a reflection in the mirror. Could be, the kid felt like a monster and wanted to run away from his family before he hurt them.

Kaitlyn skids to a stop in the doorjamb, her expression manic. "What happened?"

"Nothing. Saf's just demonstrating different screams." Ben smirks.

"Sorry, Mom." Saffron explains the situation.

"You shouldn't waste Ms. Moon's time with your imagination," says Kaitlyn.

"It's not imagination. I heard him yell." Saffron flails her arms. "You don't believe me, but I'm not making it up."

I gaze around at the exceedingly normal bedroom, frustrated at its uselessness. No clues. "Where were you when you heard him yell?"

Both parents seem a bit annoyed at me not letting it go, but there's no guilt or hostility in their eyes. I'm sure they are not trying to hide anything, merely think their daughter's imagination got the better of her and they don't want it muddling up my investigation.

"In my room." She clasps her hands in front of herself. "I thought he fell off his bed or something, but no thump."

"The scream came from in here?" I ask.

"Kinda hard to know for sure." She shrugs. "It seemed to be everywhere."

"Ms. Moon," says Ben. "I was working on the bathroom sink attached to our room when my daughter thinks she heard Milo yell. I can assure you, no sound came from his room. I don't know what she thought she heard but…"

Saffron looks down. "I'm not lying."

"Aww, sweetie…" Ben puts an arm around her. "I'm not saying you are. Just you might've imagined something that didn't really happen. Or heard a noise from outside."

J.R. RAIN AND MATTHEW S. COX

The kid gives him an 'I know what I heard' stare, but says nothing.

"What do you think?" asks Kaitlyn, looking at me.

Well, I could say that it's a damn shame I don't read minds anymore. I could just dip down into her memory and relive the scene with her. I also consider the possibility of ghosts or poltergeists. She might have heard something supernatural moving through the house. Pretty sure the family didn't want to hear that explanation, either. The odd energy around me could have something to do with spirit activity... and nothing whatsoever to do with Milo's disappearance. Or, it might have everything to do with it. Too early to say. It's also not the sort of thing I can really talk about with parents and not come off as a wingnut with some screws loose.

"It's a bit early to say anything with any degree of confidence. It's possible the yell she heard could have been him climbing out his window and losing his balance. It might have been louder in her bedroom due to an open window. For now, I'm going to start looking into the theory he's on his way to Ohio. Would you be able to give me any information on his friends there? Maybe he's made contact with them already and they're expecting his arrival."

The parents nod.

Saffron shakes her head at me.

"You don't think he ran away?" I ask.

"No." Saffron sighs.

"What do you think happened to Milo?"

The girl mulls for a moment. "I think the tooth fairy got him."

I grin. "Oh?"

"Yeah. When he lost teeth, he didn't wanna put them under his pillow. So the fairy is mad. Mom said she's gonna come back and take *all* his teeth."

Kaitlyn makes a face like she's stuck between wanting to laugh and sob. "I said that years ago. How do you even remember it? Just something silly to tease him a little over not believing in the tooth fairy."

The child's suggestion as to what happened to Milo appears to have convinced her parents to dismiss anything she has to say about it as made up... including his supposed yell. However, I can't help but dwell on the thought she might be closer to the truth than she even knows.

No, not tooth faeries. Something darker... but it does involve teeth.

Pointed ones.

Ugh, kid. C'mon. Please don't be a vampire.

Chapter Six
Gone

My head swims with depressing thoughts for the next several hours as I go from bus stop to train station to bus stop.

I keep picturing a frightened boy trying to cope with vampirism, freaking out, and pouncing a random person who stumbled across him by chance. The people at each station are helpful as they can be, willing to look at a photocopy of Milo's most recent school portrait that I brought with me to show around. No one has seen him, but they'll keep their eyes open.

By the end of hour four, I've mostly convinced myself this kid did not run away from home and try to go back to Ohio to see his friends. At least, if he did, he took an Uber. Neither his parents nor sister

think—shy of the running back to Ohio scenario—
he'd have randomly gone far without telling anyone.

Unless, of course, he'd become a vampire and
was either afraid to tell his family about it or he
didn't want to scare them. Or didn't care. I know
two things for sure at this point. One: if the kid is a
vampire, he's coming with me. Who better to watch
over a vampire child than me? Two: I really want
him not to be a vampire.

After striking out with every bus and train station close enough for a desperate thirteen-year-old
to feasibly reach by himself, I stop at the nearest
Starbucks for some latte frustration therapy and
make some phone calls to the parents of Milo's
three friends. Two put the other boys directly on the
phone with me after I explain the situation. The
third kid, Oscar, is not home. He's playing in a
youth hockey league right now. I speak with his
dad, since his mom took him to the game. Go figure, she's the sports nut and his father couldn't care
less about athletics.

Both boys and Mr. Farris—Oscar's dad—are direct and non-evasive. They all tell me Milo has not
said anything to them about plans to make his own
way back to Ohio. In fact, Charlie and Ian both cor-
roborate the opinion Milo would be too afraid of
getting in serious trouble to do something like that.
They do share that he's *not* happy about having to
move away from his friends, but they don't think

he'd run away. Too extreme. Mr. Farris even goes so far as to say he doubted Milo would 'pull a stunt like that' even if he knew the shock factor of it would absolutely convince his family to move back there.

So, yeah. I'm out of coffee and ideas by the time I'm off the phone.

As far as I'm concerned, the running away from home thing is a dead end. Nothing to it beyond parental guilt. His parents are undoubtedly second guessing themselves for deciding to move and trying to find some way to blame themselves for their son being missing.

Hate to think it, but the idea young Milo has become a bloodsucker is gaining traction in my head, if for no other reason than I've got nothing else. I'm clinging to the hope a somewhat undersized thirteen-year-old boy would be too small to make the bite marks found on the teacher. Anthony at that age would have made about the same size bite... but he's also *not* undersized for his age. Quite the opposite. Last time we went out for dinner the waiter mistook him for a grown man and offered him an alcoholic drink menu.

Thankfully, the most abnormal thing about my son isn't immortality. It's his good nature. He declined without even considering it. Sure, I happened to be sitting right there, but I have no doubt he'd have done the same thing even if he'd been on his own or with friends his age.

I discover another worry-slash-idea at the bottom of my empty coffee cup: abduction.

The yelp Saffron heard *might* have come from someone surprising Milo and dragging him out of his bedroom window. It's definitely a long shot-slash-unlikely possibility. He's still a kid, but a boy his age would make a ton of noise if someone they didn't want to go with grabbed them. It would be much more difficult for a single adult to physically abscond with a thirteen-year-old and not have a struggle on their hands.

No, yanking a kid his age out a window silently would require multiple people and the precision of a SWAT team. Something tells me that's laughable here. Maybe Milo really did sneak out of the house with the intent to go back to Ohio, but he slipped and fell out the window. That might explain the yell.

Anxiety boils over in my gut. One thing that totally sucks about being a little psychic is it's no longer obvious to me when random feelings are more significant than me worrying myself to death. Grr. There's a missing kid, and he's already been gone for two days. After forty-eight hours, statistically, the odds of finding them alive are bleak. Sure, oddities happen, but I'm not going to sit back and trust fate to throw me a bone.

Time to cheat.

I call Allison.

"Sam…" she says rather sleepily. "Do you

know what time it is?"

"Almost six in the evening," I say to my friend, who works the night shift. "You should have been awake for a few hours. Stop messing with me."

She grumbles. "Bah. You're no fun."

"Sorry... serious time. Missing kid. I need your help."

"Eep!"

I picture her going from draped on the couch to sitting bolt upright in an instant. "Yeah, eep indeed. Gone without a trace."

"Oh, I hate those. What's his name?"

She's already picked up on the fact he's a boy, a good sign. "Milo Boone. Age thirteen."

"Runaway?"

"Possible, but I'm kinda doubting that for some reason I can't quite put my finger on." I fidget at the empty Starbucks cup while explaining everything I've learned so far. "Any possibility you can distant view him or somehow find him? Oh, there's another... uhh, possibility."

"What?"

I glance around. Too many people here waiting for coffee or drinking it... so I leave and start walking to my minivan. "Sherbet pulled me in on a strange homicide case yesterday. Looks like the result of a new vampire losing control."

"You think this kid might be a vamp now?"

"Maybe it's my fear getting the better of me, but I can't stop myself from going down that mental path. The bite mark seemed a touch on the small side. Not 'child' small, but definitely not an adult man or woman."

She emits this sad gurgling 'oh no' kind of noise. "Okay. I'll see what I can pick up on. Umm, can you email me a photo of Milo? Maybe drop off a personal item? I need *something* to focus on."

"Yeah, I got a photo on me now." I tap my foot. Do I tell the parents I'm involving a psychic and ask for something personal of his… or simply teleport to his bedroom and help myself?

My brother Dusk had this philosophy growing up: it's easier to ask for forgiveness than permission. I don't think the Bloom family would care about the psychic thing if and when Milo is home safe and sound. Besides, they won't know some random item got borrowed for a few hours.

I set the empty paper cup inside the Momvan, close my eyes, and call the dancing flame—picturing Milo's bedroom. Through the little hole in the fire, it's obvious there's no one in the room at the moment. Perfect. The van can wait here for now.

Allie's gotta be able to find him.

Chapter Seven
Overdue Process

The most guaranteed way for something *not* to work is me wanting it to.

Allison had some difficulty getting a vision while focusing on Milo's picture or his PlayStation controller. It seemed a logical choice given it's one of the few items he'd unpacked. Plus, according to his sister, he loved the time they spent together playing games.

Loves, dammit. Not 'loved.' Grr, brain, stop it. Milo isn't dead.

While most of everything about my change to a psychic vampire is awesome, there are still occasional times when being an undead vampire had its benefits. For example: sleeping. Sunrise used to knock me clean out no matter how worried/

anxious/upset/angry I was. Last night? No sleep. None. Zero. Just me and Judge Judy all damn night. Fortunately, in my present state, I can go a while without sleep if need be.

It's 1:33 p.m. Wednesday. Tammy's here at the office since she got out of school early, thanks to her light senior schedule. She decided to come here and help out rather than hang with her friends. My daughter is presently making phone calls wherever she can think to in an effort to find any information about Milo's disappearance. I spent the morning going back to all the bus stations and even widened my search, wondering if Milo might've hitchhiked or taken a ride service to a more distant train station. No, I don't think he put that much effort into trying to avoid being found, but I got nothing else.

And yeah, *nothing* is all we got. We have heaps of nothing. It's almost like this kid fell through a hole in reality and simply ceased existing.

Even if a team of commandos yanked him out of his window, there'd be more evidence than we've seen. It's almost like he never left his house… or he really was a vampire. If my worst-case scenario theory is accurate, he might be horrified at having killed the teacher and is hiding out somewhere, terrified of getting in trouble and guilt-ridden.

I simmer in my chair for a while, thoroughly unable to come up with any ideas of more to do for this kid other than wait for Allison to call me with some better news. She said something about having to break out the big guns, e.g. crystals, for this one. Ugh. Not sure if it's a bad sign or simply a complication from her not having a direct connection to the subject of the viewing. Meaning, she's not on the phone talking to him. Working from a photo and whatever emotional attachment the kid infused into his game controller is, apparently, more difficult for her than a phone connection.

Need to do *something* other than sit here feeling useless and clueless. I frown at the blue paper on the desk. Might as well try to do that process serve Tammy backed out of. Again, not criticizing her. She needs to trust her instincts.

"Back in a bit... gonna try that process thing. Need to do something," I say while standing and swiping the documents up.

"Okay. Still nothing here." Tammy sighs. "How's Allie doing?"

"She's working on it." I start for the door.

"Cool. I'll call you if I find anything."

"Thanks, Tam." I pause at the door. "You gonna be okay here?"

She pulls a giant can of pepper spray out of her desk drawer and sets it next to the keyboard with a firm clank. "Yep."

"Unless you'd rather come with?"

Tammy tilts her head, thinks for half a second, then tosses the pepper spray back in the drawer. "Yeah. I'll hang back and video record it in case the guy tries to say he never got the paperwork."

"Good idea." I wait for her to scoot out the door, flip the sign to 'back soon – out on a case' and lock the door.

***

We take Tammy's Prius.

Better she drive anyway since my mind is going in worry circles over Milo.

Tammy provides the perfect distraction on the ride to Buena Park. About the only thing that could make me stop thinking/worrying about a missing child is something happening to one of my kids. Anthony apparently got into a 'fight' at school to-day. Though, the semantics of 'fight' is a stretch. A couple of jocks decided to pick on another boy for being small and nerdy. Ant told them to knock it off and when they didn't, he picked a kid up with a one-handed grip on his shirt, pressed him to the wall and said something to the effect of, "I said, leave him alone."

No one got hit or hurt.

The bully accused Anthony of 'shoving him into the wall' but, according to Tammy, the school isn't doing anything because enough witnesses said he was standing up for the smaller kid, not initiating a fight. So, there's that. It must have been serious, meaning that Anthony believed those boys would cause harm to the other kid, for him to 'show off' his strength like that.

Generally, we try to keep things as outwardly normal as possible. I think my son knows things now. Like... even if those boys weren't about to inflict serious injury to the other kid, he must have been worried they might have eventually tormented him to the point of suicide or something. I'm sure Ant can sense weird stuff like that, though he doesn't say much about it. He wanted to step in before it escalated to that level. At least, it would explain why he resorted to an overt display of strength to scare the bully into leaving the smaller boy alone.

I'm not quite done processing the story when we arrive at the address. Desmond Carter, the man to whom I need to deliver these papers, lives on the third floor of an apartment building. For this part of Southern California, it's not the nicest area in terms of crime, but it's 'affordable.' A few locals are hanging around outside, but don't pay much attention to us as we leave the car and go into the building's lobby.

Two flights of stairs later, we're in the hallway approaching his door. My warning bells don't go off. This is good. Tammy hangs back about five paces, pointing her phone at me and the door. My plan is pretty simple. Knock, wait for him to open said door, then just hand him the papers. The vast majority of people will reflexively grab/clutch an object shoved toward them. Mission accomplished.

I knock.

And wait.

And listen.

Total silence inside.

I close my eyes and reach out my mental feelers, pushing through the door and into the messy apartment beyond. It's a handy trick that may or may not be a by-product of Elizabeth's doing. More likely, it's part of my 'feeding mechanism.' Makes sense that a psychic vampire would be able to sense the presence of living minds nearby from which to draw energy. Or, it might just be my soul's need to temporarily bust out of the limited confines of this physical body. At any rate, no one's inside. Not even a cat.

"No one there," I mutter. "Place is empty."

"Think he's hiding?" Tammy lowers her phone.

"Inside, no. Somewhere else... yeah, probably."

"He might be at his brother's place. There's a sister listed, too, but I don't think he'd be there."

I raise both eyebrows. "Why not?"

"She has a restraining order on him," deadpans Tammy. "Guessing they're not on good terms."

"Oh, that's right." I shake my head. Not too often you see a sister getting a restraining order against her brother.

We leave the apartment building and drive to where the brother, Lenny Carter, lives. He's got a tiny house, maybe a third the size of mine, which is saying something. It's basically a living room with an attached bedroom and a toilet closet squeezed in between them. The yard's unkempt. Not to infer anything about Lenny's activities here, but in passing, it looks kinda like a crack house... or a pot den.

Tammy did a brief background check on Lenny just in case she had to pay him a visit, too. Bunch of minor arrests for drug charges, no violence. Again, she hangs back while I approach the door and knock.

A little over a minute later, a gruff male voice calls out from the other side of the door without opening it. "Go away."

"Lenny?" I ask.

"I said, go away. Don't care what you want."

"I'm trying to find your brother, Desmond. It's important."

"Get fucked," yells Lenny.

Tammy whistles. "Not the friendliest sort of guy, is he?"

"Do you know where Desmond is?" I ask.

No response.

Okay, tough guy. Two can play this game. This time I use I let my brain vacuum off its leash, so to speak, using the same sense that allows me to feed on nearby psychic energy. Only one sentient mind in the house. Gotta be Lenny. I siphon off enough energy from him to where he enjoys an impromptu nap wherever he happened to be standing or sitting. A soft *thud* confirms he'd been standing.

There. I feel better. Petty, but, necessary. Better this than me taking out my frustrations over the

Milo situation on this guy simply for cursing at me. Can't blame him for wanting to protect his brother from the legal system, but it's still annoying.

"No luck?" asks Tammy.

"Nope. He's not here. Just Lenny."

Tammy turns to walk back to the Prius. "I thought you lost your telepathy."

"I did… mostly." Once we're back in the car, I remind her that I still have my internal radar system that lets me push through walls and doors—and even through bedrock once when looking for the entrance to the underground L.A. River system... where I eventually witnessed Danny getting killed.

I leave out that last part. As much as Danny was a dick to me in the end, the guy still loved his kids in his own way. And hadn't he been the voice of reason in Anthony's ear for a few years when hiding out in my son's mind?

He had. And, yes... my life is weird.

Mostly, I explain how my current nature—feeding off psychic energy—allows me to also sense people's presence. No, I can't tell what they're thinking or talk to them, but it's impossible for a living person to hide from me. If they are within about 100 feet, I know they exist. It's almost like I'm seeing brain-sized azure lights hovering in the dark.

"Neat," says Tammy in reaction to my description. "What now?"

"Might as well talk to the sister. If she's not on

friendly terms with Desmond, she'd be prone to helping us."

Tammy wags her head side to side in thought. "I dunno. If she's afraid of him, she might not want to help us."

"True, but we can at least try. This guy is only dodging child support. Not like he's on the run from the feds for being a serial killer."

"Right? Don't say that." She gives me side eye. "No one is thought of as a serial killer until they're caught. Then everyone's all shocked it was *that* guy they knew for years."

I stare at her. "You think so?"

"Nah. This guy's too lazy and disorganized. Just saying."

***

Heather Carter also lives in an apartment, though she's in Anaheim.

The place isn't ritzy, but it's clean and nice. Definitely a better area than where her older brother ended up. A mid-thirties woman with brown hair in teal scrubs answers the door when I knock. No ID badge or anything, so she could be anything from a vet tech to a dental hygienist to a nurse to a cosplaying singing telegram performer. Considering she's home at about three in the afternoon, I'm guessing she either just got off shift or she's about to go on.

My immediate impression of her is fairly normal. Not particularly mousy, fearful, aggressive, or hostile.

"Umm, are you at the right place?" asks Heather.

"Heather Carter?" I ask.

She tenses. "Uhh, yeah. What's this about?"

"I'm not a cop or a salesperson, I swear." I smile, hold up my private investigator license. It's an old picture, taken back when I was a blood vamp, which is why there's so much damn makeup on my face. Only way I could show up on film. "I'm a PI trying to find your brother Desmond to give him some legal documents."

Heather grimaces. "Oh, he hates that. Last time a guy tried to give him one of those, he almost ran him over."

Tammy shivers. Her instincts with this guy were spot on. Good girl.

"I can deal with whatever your brother comes up with," I say, shrugging.

She regards me with a bit of a 'yeah sure, okay' smirk, but doesn't slam the door in my face. "I don't know where he is. He won't come around here, that's for sure. At least, he better not."

"Yes, I am aware there's a protection order in effect."

Heather fidgets. "Yeah."

"I understand if you're concerned he might re-taliate against you if you help me find him. It's all right. I'm not going to ask you to put yourself in danger." I take a step back. "We'll find him, eventually."

"Oh, it's not that." She shakes her head. "Telling you where he is won't make anything worse. He already wants to kill me."

Tammy coughs.

"Sorry…" I grimace. "He tried to kill you?"

"Yeah. He convinced the cops he was just frustrated, but I know him. He's manipulative… and legitimately nuts. Like, a psychopath, but he's never been diagnosed. Desmond avoids doctors. He thinks I tried to get him put away for being crazy and made our parents afraid of him… so he wants to get revenge."

Tammy edges closer to me, looks over her shoulder.

"I haven't seen him in person for, I dunno… six years?" Heather rakes a hand up through her hair. "He wouldn't come here to hide, and if he did, I'd have already called the police. I know he's got a friend, Colby or something, in Buena Park. He lives somewhere around Ninth Street, I think."

"Colby?" I ask, just to keep the name at the tip of my brain while I get my phone out to create a note. "Any idea what the last name is?"

"Umm, not really. Smalls? Smith maybe. Something with an S," says Heather. "It's definitely Colby, though."

"Okay. Thank you." I smile and offer one of my cards. "If you do happen to hear something about

where he is, please call me. I'm only trying to deliver court documents. Again, not a cop."

She takes the card, glances at it, then nods. "I
understand. But… Desmond can be unreasonable,
and… unpredictable."

"Violent?" asks Tammy.

"Yes. It's definitely possible." Heather tenses
again. "When he told me I was going to regret causing trouble for him, he went straight for a knife in
the kitchen."

"He attacked you?" I ask, somewhat surprised.

"I ran like hell. He didn't get the chance to do
anything with it." She shoots a dark look off to one
side. "Tried to claim I was lying about the knife, but
Dad saw it happen. Desmond's angry with Dad, too,
but he's afraid of him for some reason. Our dad's
the most calm, nice guy you can imagine. Guess
Des is stuck thinking about him like a little boy.
When dads are all powerful, you know?"

"Right." I exhale. "Thanks for your help."

"Hey, um. I didn't want to say anything, but if
you're involved in some kind of custody or child
support type case…" Heather leans out of her doorway, peering around as if to make sure Desmond
isn't spying on us. "If he loses, there's a really good
chance he will try to hurt his kids, or his ex-wife…
or all of them. Please tell them to be careful."

"Eep," whispers Tammy.

Great. I suppress the urge to stare into the sky.
This 'simple' process serve is getting complicated.

Still, it's easier to deal with than the possibility of a young man turning into a vampire before he's even shaved once.

I thank Heather, and we head back to the Prius. If I'd been trying to find Desmond for something more pressing than a document serve, I'd probably start canvassing his workplace. We have a potential friend's name, but I'll need more than a vague last name and 'somewhere around Ninth Street' to go on first.

Back to the office it is.

C'mon, Allie. Call... tell me where Milo is.

Chapter Eight
On Call

It's Wednesday night. I'm at home. It's dinner-time.

Getting too wrapped up in my work isn't usually a problem for me… except when my work involves a missing child who might have become a vampire. Bad enough there's a young boy out there, fate unknown. The added problem of the supernatural adds an exponentially more complicated layer of *argh*. I'm worried about Milo enough to not have the ability to truly enjoy this time with my family.

Paxton and Anthony are talking about seeing a 'vampire attack' on the news. It's the teacher Sherbet found. As they so often do, the news media is trying to spin it up for ratings, playing to the sensationalist nature of it. Of course, they're not sincerely suggesting a vampire is on the loose, merely an ordinary killer with a flair for the theatrical.

While they talk about the news, my thoughts wander around how I'm going to handle the 'Milo is a vampire' situation. Three options rise to the top of the list of most plausible...

One: I tell the parents exactly the truth and let them decide if he should stay with them or let me essentially foster him. Considering I can't wipe out memories anymore, this option has the potential to be quite bad if they don't take the news well.

Option two: I find Milo but tell the parents he's gone without a trace, then relocate the boy to another state well out of reach of accidental discovery. Something tells me the kid wouldn't react well to this. Bad enough he's been dragged away from his friends and familiar surroundings in Ohio. Having to lose his family on top of that would only make it worse.

Option three: I take him home with me and keep him without telling the parents anything.

Yeah, I know. Not a great idea.

Ugh. I had enough trouble dealing with making my son momentarily a vampire. Oh, hang on. Maybe there's an option four... could there be another diamond medallion out there somewhere? I'd only have to keep Milo out of sight until I could find the means to return him to human.

Sure. Yeah. Those things fall off trees. I'll just pop over to Walmart and pick up four. You know, to keep a few extras on hand so I don't have to run to the store again the next time one is needed. Dammit, Sam. Ancient, powerful alchemical artifacts aren't bar soap. Considering one of those medallions as part of my plan is about as ridiculous as planning to win the lottery.

Wait... did Fang ever actually use the diamond medallion? I'm pretty sure he had it last. Did he give it to someone else or use it on them? Used it on another? Hard to know. Like I said, a potential option four. Hmm. He *might* still have it.

"Do you think it's a real vampire, Mom?" asks Paxton.

"Real ones aren't that careless." Tammy shakes her head. "It's probably a nutjob like the news guy said."

"Mom?" Paxton tilts her head at me, eyebrows ever so slightly raised. "You're upset. And sad. Wanna talk about it?"

"She thinks the missing boy we're trying to find has become a vampire," deadpans Tammy.

"Oh, no." Paxton gasps. "He's not old enough. Is he gonna get in trouble?"

Anthony smiles to himself the way he does whenever Pax says or does something naïve and/or cute.

Tammy chuckles. "Pax, it's undeath, not sneaking into an R-rated movie. I don't think he had a choice."

I give her side eye. "You think he's the vampire,

too?"

"Not exactly." Tammy shrugs one shoulder. "Just saying. If he is, it wouldn't be anything he wanted."

"Is it ever?" mutters Anthony.

My son isn't exactly upset or sad about the course our life took, but I do think part of him would not have minded if we'd have been entirely normal, either.

"Oh." Paxton exhales in a 'yeah, okay, that was dumb of me' sort of way. "I hope he's not the vampire."

"Same," I say.

"Spent all day calling around." Tammy grumbles. "No trace. If this kid isn't a vampire, the CIA has him hidden away somewhere in Panama."

"What's in Panama?" asks Anthony.

"Nothing. Just picking a random foreign country that sounds like a place the CIA might operate a black op site." Tammy laughs.

I know I'm in a bad mood when the urge to snap at my daughter for laughing while a boy is missing almost makes it out of my mouth. Fortunately, I stop myself. No point starting a useless argument. At any given time in the world, there have to be thousands of children missing. If people had to be grim out of respect for all of them, we'd all be in a perpetual state of misery.

And on that cheerful note, my phone rings.

I jump, hopeful it might be a random ticket clerk

at a bus station or maybe one of the State Police barracks I contacted between here and Ohio calling to follow up because they've found Milo. I dismiss that idea almost as soon as it hits me. Cops would call the parents first, not some random private investigator. Unless... they found Milo's *body* and had no idea who his parents are.

Ugh. Dammit!

Thankfully, it's only Detective Sherbet.

When I answer the phone, Tammy and Anthony give me 'the look.' It's the stare they give me every time I break the rule of 'no phones at dinnertime.' Paxton's reaction to the rule was 'okay.' Unlike the other two, she didn't complain.

"It's Detective Sherbet," I say while moving the phone to my ear.

Both kids go from accusing stares to 'okay, fine' expressions.

"I hope you have some good news," I say by way of answering.

"Afraid not, Sam." Sherbet sighs. "There's another body. I'm at the scene now. Just got here. Looks pretty similar. Hoping you might be available to come earn some of that consultant pay."

I'd chuckle, but someone just died. "Yeah, I can do that. Where?"

He gives me an intersection off West Mountain View Ave in La Habra. Not too far from here to the north.

"You're leaving?" asks Paxton in a slightly disappointed but not upset tone.

"Cop stuff," whispers Tammy. "It's important."

I stare at the little bit of chicken and potato on my plate. Thankfully, he managed to wait until we were nearly done before he called. Not like I *just* sat down and hadn't touched my food yet. "I'm on the way."

The fifteen seconds it takes me to scarf the last few mouthfuls won't hurt anyone.

Especially not the dead guy.

Chapter Nine
Crime Scene

It's always a pain to find a decent parking spot at a crime scene.

To avoid the headache since it's dark outside and relatively close to home, I decide to fly. The collection of police vehicles creates a flickering, glimmering beacon visible from the sky for miles. Most of the cars gather in a parking lot next to a blue and white building. Sherbet's standing toward the back of the property, by an area enclosed in chain link fence. Looks like a storage spot containing pallets of tile or something and a big steel cargo box.

I land in an empty dirt lot across the street from the place where it's pretty dark. Anyone in the area likely to see me drop out of the sky would almost certainly have their attention monopolized by the swarm of police. After pulling out my cute little 'consultant badge' and letting it dangle around my neck, I head over to meet Sherbet.

"Thanks for coming." He smiles. "You got here pretty fast. Coroner hasn't even shown up yet."

"Yeah, traffic was light. I really flew."

He smirks at my pun, the only one among all the officers here to get my true meaning. "Any luck so far?" he asks in a hushed tone.

"Not yet." I lower my voice so only he can hear me. "Whoever we're looking for, they're proving to be suspiciously elusive. It's beyond strange. Maybe I'm thinking along the wrong track."

"How so?" He raises an eyebrow as he starts leading me toward the body.

On the short walk into the fenced-in area, I explain the Milo Boone situation and my worry he might be the vampire in question.

"Yeah, that does seem kinda strange. Kids that age don't usually vanish without leaving at least *some* signs of their passage."

I nod, then glance down when we stop beside a dead man. He's slumped against a pallet of small cinder blocks, the kind people make decorative garden walls out of. Someone walking by on the street might've mistaken him for a sleeping homeless guy due to the casualness of his pose, if not for him looking markedly too clean and neat to be a vagrant. That, and, not many people use concrete blocks for pillows.

As is his usual habit, Sherbet says nothing to avoid tainting my perception of the scene. I put on some blue nitrile gloves and begin to pretend to be a forensic tech. This guy appears to be around fifty, give or take two in either direction. He's thin. Too thin, and smells rather strongly—to me—of inexpensive pine-infused soap. I spot a few tiny hairs stuck to his forehead and the side of his face. They look like his, suggesting a recent haircut. A few red spots on the face also indicate he shaved. However, the cuts didn't bleed. My guess is the killer cleaned him up after the fact.

The man is wearing a pea-soup-green button-down shirt and business casual pants in light beige. His shoes are those mutant half-sneaker, half-hiking-boot things. They appear well-worn, but this guy doesn't look like an outdoorsy type. Well, I mean… if one considers homeless people 'outdoorsy,' he'd fit. Add long hair and a shaggy, unkempt beard. My suspicion deepens upon examination of his teeth—at least as much as possible, given the stiffness of his skin. His mouth is a disaster.

Working my way down...

Two neat puncture wounds align with the carotid artery in his neck. I study them, shifting around to get as close a look as possible. Unlike the teacher, these bite marks are pristine. No ripping, no bruising, near perfect circles.

"Not gonna bite him again, are you?" asks Sherbet—totally kidding.

"Nope. He's a bit undercooked."

Sherbet chuckles.

This body has a conspicuous lack of claw wounds. Without undressing him, the only marks on the body in sight are the fang punctures. I don't have a ruler on me, but eyeballing it, the bite looks as though someone larger made it than the one on Joseph Keeley. The fangs responsible for this bite would have to be attached to an adult man. Also, the bite would have had to happen while the victim was unconscious… or already dead.

"So, what do you think?" asks Sherbet.

"Well…" I look up from the wound and glance around the area. Nothing appears to be disturbed to indicate a struggle or chase happened here, nor do I see any blood. "My guess is this man was killed somewhere else. Rigor's starting to set in. Can't really see through his shirt, but I'm going to assume the livor mortis won't match his present reclining pose."

Sherbet shifts his jaw side to side. "Had that feeling as well, but I'm mostly asking about the more odd aspects of the deceased."

I stand and take a step back from the body, ending up beside Sherbet. "If a vampire did this, it's not the same one… unless they grew up from thirteen to thirty in a matter of days. Or… transformed from a small woman to a large man."

"Hear the doctors in Sweden are doing crazy

things these days," says Sherbet.

"Not this crazy. Something isn't adding up."

"Just one thing?" He raises both eyebrows.

I gesture at the body's feet. "Going to bet when the medical examiner gets his shoes off, he's going to find a horror show in there."

"How do you mean? His feet?" Sherbet gives me a perplexed stare.

"The guy smells like soap. There's evidence of a recent haircut and postmortem shave. His clothes are awfully clean and don't really fit him too well. I think this is a homeless guy the killer doesn't want us to realize was homeless. Cleaned him up after death."

Sherbet goes to rub his chin, eyes the blue glove, and hesitates. "That *does* explain the lack of wallet or ID on him. So why would a killer prey on a vagrant and then make him look *not* like a vagrant?"

I mull that for a moment. "Maybe because they want the case to get attention, not be back burnered?"

"We don't ignore dead vagrants," grumbles Sherbet.

"I know that. The killer doesn't. Perhaps he's cynical." I wave randomly. "Kill a guy no one will miss or some might even be glad to be rid of, the cops naturally don't give it the attention they'd give a wealthy citizen."

"Yeah, yeah." He sets his hands on his hips,

frowning.

"Though, that idea means this killer is playing games. Taunting the cops. Wants to be famous." I tap my foot. "I also don't think this is a vampire's work."

Sherbet gives me side eye. "How's that?"

"The fang marks are too clean. They're also perfectly aligned with the carotid artery. That's like the vampire equivalent of someone with OCD who has to cut their turkey dinner into exactly one-inch squares before they can eat it. Also, the fang wounds seem to have been inflicted postmortem as well. My kids were talking about the news. The dead teacher's been going around as a vampire story."

"Ugh. Don't get me started." Sherbet glares at the clouds. "Those people make it hard to do my job sometimes."

"Those people?" I ask, raising an eyebrow. The phrase tends to get a bad reaction from some.

"Journalists. I mean… I get it. They're doing their job. News has to be reported, but they always have to spin things sensationalist." He holds his hands up, waving his fingers. "Ooh, there's a vampire around."

I nod. "Yeah. Could be someone teetering on the verge of experimenting with murder saw that and got inspired."

"A copycat?"

"Yeah, maybe."

"Kind of a stretch, no?" Sherbet fidgets. "Unless that was like a psychic hit or something."

"Or something. Might just be my overactive imagination." I point at the body. "Can you ask the ME to check those fang marks and see if they can tell what sort of implement made them? An actual tooth or something metal?"

"Can ask. No idea if they will be able to." He wanders around to the north side of the body. "Smell a blood trail?"

"Not anymore. I'm a psychic vampire now, re-member?"

"Oh, right. That makes a difference?"

"It does when it comes to blood. Hmm."

"Hmm?" He blinks. "You got something?"

"Not yet." I crouch beside the body again and gently rest a hand on his arm. "Hoping for some luck of the unexplainable kind."

A few seconds after making contact with intent to 'read,' an unusual mood comes over me. For no reason whatsoever, my emotions shift without a clutch. I'm full of adoration and excitement. Not good excitement, though. It's the malignant sort of thrill someone gets while doing something they shouldn't be doing and getting away with it. The sensation is repulsive enough to where I jerk my hand back as if touching a hot stove.

The strange mood evaporates in an instant, proving it came from a psychic hit.

It's not admissible in any courtroom, but I am

certain now whoever killed this man did it not to feed but for the rush. Sherbet might've been onto something about a copycat killer.

"This is off the record," I whisper. "The killer was thrilled with what they did. Not getting any sense of hunger. Doubt it was a vampire. We've got two bodies with two different killers."

"Damn." Sherbet kicks his toe at the parking lot surface.

A spot of pink catches my eye on the ground across the street behind a cluster of giant plastic trash cans. They're positioned near a big brown garage door in the tan building facing this parking lot. I'm not sure why a small pink object struck me as so significant it pulled me away from my focus on the body. But... it did.

Must be psychic.

"One second..." I walk away from the dead guy, ignoring the arriving medical examiner's van, cross the street, and approach the trash cans.

Sherbet follows, no doubt curious as hell what's gotten my eye.

Something more than the sight of this spot of bright color is pulling me there. A feeling of significance goes with it. Either my brain or the universe at large wants me to see this. No sense arguing. Crossing the street only wastes a couple minutes if it's nothing.

The pink ends up being a Hello Kitty rubber keychain attachment. It's looped to a small assortment of common keys, along with a clear pouch that holds a plastic card like some hotels use for their door systems. A small patch of exposed dirt behind the trash cans also contains footprints. It shouldn't be possible for me to tell simply by looking at sneaker tracks in dirt, but for some reason I just *know* a person was crouching there, hiding. It also hits me that this person probably witnessed the killer leaving the body. The spectacle likely spooked them so badly they ran off as soon as they could and forgot their keys.

"Check this out." I point. "Someone was hiding here. Bet they saw the guy dump the body."

Sherbet glances back at the fenced-in storage area, then back to where we're standing. "Kinda far away."

Careful not to step on the footprints, I position myself in roughly the same pose I feel the person was in and try to look toward the dead guy. Can't see him from here. But… if he'd been lugged out of a trunk, he would've been visible until placed on the ground. "They would have seen enough. I'm sure of it."

"More psychic woo?"

"Yeah, kinda."

"Ugh. Sam…" Sherbet rubs a hand over his head in frustration. "You know I can't do much with it."

"Not officially, but you can use it to lead you to other, more concrete, evidence." I smile at him.

"You call me in, you have to be expecting a little woo. The normal stuff, you can handle."

Sherbet eyes the keyring. "So, we might have a potential witness. Or that crap's been sitting there for days."

Since I'm still wearing gloves, I gently pick up the keys, remove the hotel card from the plastic sleeve. The card is old, worn at the edges, and faded. Text used to be on it, but it's gone. Only a small 'Aladdin's lamp' icon remains. A hint of cheap perfume clings to the rubber figurine. I hold the card up so Sherbet can see it. "Any idea what this symbol means?"

"Not off the top of my head. I can ask around, though."

"Fingerprints?"

"Unlikely, but c'mon over to the car and I can give it a shot." He starts walking back to his grey sedan. "Any woo here, by the way?"

"Only insofar as it feels significant to me." I shrug. "Probably means whoever was hiding there had nothing to do with the killing other than being a witness to the body dumping. Then again, this psychometry thing is new to me. Not sure that even counts as psychometry. Might be straight up clairvoyance."

"I ain't got time to learn a new language, Sam." Sherbet chuckles. "No idea what you're talking about."

While I *could* explain to him that *psychometry* is

the psychic skill of being able to read emotions and memories out of objects... and *clairvoyance* is a more general psychic ability to see and feel things about one's environment, he's not sincerely asking for clarification.

Sherbet pulls a kit from his trunk and dusts the keyring. One clear print, maybe a thumb, on the card gives hope. He preserves it and sticks the tape in a protective baggy. "This is a long shot, Sam. We'd have to get incredibly lucky for a random potential witness to even have their print in the system. If they weren't in the military or an ex-con, all we're going to be able to do with this print is hang onto it for future comparison."

"I know. But... a long shot is more than what we have now."

"I hate that you're right." Sherbet closes the fingerprinting kit, then whispers, "If you can do any psychic crap to find this guy, go right ahead. I'd appreciate you leading me to him, but if it's a question of take him out or he kills again, you know what to do."

I smile. "Yep. Knock him senseless, then call you."

Sherbet grins. "Pleasure working with you."

"Same."

He tosses me the keyring. "You might as well hang onto this, in case it lights up your woo woo senses again."

I snatch it out of the air, stare at the rubberized

Hello Kitty figurine. It's the sort of thing Paxton would adore. Can't give her this one, but maybe I'll pick a new one up for her.

And if I can track down the hotel with the Aladdin lamp logo, I might just find out who this keyring belongs to.

Easier said than done.

Chapter Ten
Waiting Game

Thursday is awash in worry.

Allison still hasn't gotten back to me about Milo. This means any visions she's been able to get gave her nothing useful, or she hasn't seen anything. On one hand, this is a fairly good clue nothing extreme has happened to the boy. The more desperate his circumstances, the more likely he'd have thrown psychic energy out into the world she could have picked up on. I convince myself to take her non-contact thus far as a sign of hope.

After the kids leave for school, I decide to distract myself from endless, circular worrying by doing the one thing on my plate with a concrete path to follow: the process serve from hell. Desmond's sister hinted that he might be violently mentally ill.

Tammy managed to track down the best friend based on the information we got. At least, we think so. There's a record of a guy named Colby Shaw living on Ninth Street in Buena Park. Heather didn't remember the friend's last name beyond it starting with an S. However, 'Colby' is a relatively unique name. The odds of there being two Colbys living on Ninth Street are pretty damn remote.

Least I can do is talk to this one.

And yeah, my daughter is getting darn good at this detecting business. She got a few "atta girls" from me, even as I secretly worried she might be getting *too* good at this stuff.

Like, following in her mother's footsteps and forgoing college kind of good.

Anyway, in much the same way that Milo's house hit me with a heavy, obvious sense of weirdness, the apartment building—heck, the whole development—gives me bad vibes. It's not otherworldly, like at the Boone house. No, this is definitely quite worldly and normal. I'm in an area better off avoided by out-of-towners. The weight of multiple pairs of eyes on me, no doubt lookouts trying to determine if I'm a cop or not, is as obvious as the odor of meth and marijuana in the air. To be fair, my sense of smell is a bit over-tuned compared to normal people.

Hmm. It's been like fourteen years since I carried valid federal credentials. Do I still give off 'cop vibes'? Maybe, but the locals would probably be confused about me being alone. Even detectives usually work in pairs, especially when visiting the less reputable parts of the city.

I approach the door to Colby's apartment, which sits behind a small concrete porch at the end of a short sidewalk spur. Two square patches of bare dirt —they may have been lawns in years past—stand on either side, strewn with various bits of debris: litter, plus the remnants of an old grill and some smashed plastic patio furniture and at least one Styrofoam cooler. This is the sort of neighborhood where pizza delivery people just sorta Frisbee the pie out the window of their car at the door without coming to a full stop.

The phrase 'has seen better days' definitely applies to this building. It falls short of qualifying as 'run down,' but it's far from being in great shape. Suppose the best thing to be said about it is the rain likely doesn't leak inside. A living room type window to the right of the door offers no clue as to what goes on inside thanks to a combination of opaque grime and yellowing curtains.

That said, three men are inside—I can hear them talking about some video game as well as sports. Cartoony gunfire and other explosive sound effects frequently drown out their voices. I stand there for a minute or two listening, though none of them address each other by name. Having never met Desmond Carter, I can't recognize his voice, but I think he's here. Call it a hunch.

Okay, game time.

I push the doorbell, but nothing happens. Figures. I knock.

The video game sounds stop, as does the conversation.

A moment later, a skinny fortyish black guy in sweat pants and a tank top opens the door enough to peer out at me as if he's ready to jump back behind the slab of wood and take cover against a potential gunfight. Instinct tells me he's holding a gun but keeping it out of sight. Thankfully, I'm not too worried about gunshots these days, so it's not difficult for me to pretend to be oblivious of the danger a weapon would pose to an ordinary person.

"Hi," I say. "I'm trying to find Desmond Carter. Is he here?"

The man looks me over, his expression midway between checking me out and assessing what sort of potential threat I could be. "I ain't no Desmond."

"I didn't say you were. No, you're Colby Shaw, of course. His friend." I offer a faint smile. "Relax. I'm just a courier"—I hold up the paperwork—"got a delivery for him."

Colby attempts to 'pff' dismissively and roll his eyes. "Nah, girl. He ain't here. Haven't seen him in a couple weeks."

"Are you sure?" I raise an eyebrow. "Could have sworn I heard you talking to him."

"Just a game." Colby nods toward the interior of his apartment. "Voices in a game. I'm alone. Ain't know where he went."

And with that, he shuts the door.

Well, crap. Since I'm not a SWAT team serving a search warrant—merely a PI attempting to serve a subpoena—there's no booting in the door. So, I do the only thing within my legal reach at the moment and pretend to leave. As I turn my back on the door, my inner alarm pings once, loudly. It's a 'hurry up and get going' sort of ping... not so much an imminent harm warning.

Yeah, good thing Tammy decided to back off on this one. Six steps later, I'm back on the sidewalk and the sense of alarm fades away. Most likely, someone came close to attacking me but changed their mind. Between my gut feeling and what Heather told me, my guess is Desmond—not Colby—contemplated attacking me. No way for me to know if walking away stopped him or if maybe his friends held him back. I do know one thing, however. When the time comes for me to finally confront him face to face, there is an expectation of violence. I'll need to keep my guard up.

I walk to the end of the block, go around the corner, then—once I'm sure no one is watching me—fly over the apartment complex to the roof of the building facing Colby's. Like some sort of California Girl version of a gargoyle, I perch behind a fake chimney or whatever this thing is, and watch the door.

My hope is that Desmond will, realizing he's

been found, wait a reasonable amount of time for me to leave the area and then flee in search of a new, unknown hiding place. All I need to do is catch him out in public. Not like I'm trying to arrest him or anything. I merely need to hand him a fat envelope. It would be best to get the handoff on video so there is proof of his being served the legal documents. I'll have to try to jockey my phone out quick once he makes a run for it. Without video, he can try to claim he never got the documents. It's merely a waste of time. One can't dodge the courts indefinitely.

So, there I sit, hoping ol' Desmond is not the most patient sort of person.

Telling Colby I heard him inside was intentional. I wanted Desmond to know that I know he's there. Really doesn't make sense to me why this guy is going to such extreme lengths to avoid a domestic subpoena. It's not like I'm a federal marshal looking to drag him off to prison.

Gonna go out on a limb here and say at least part of the reason he's not been paying child support is the dude has no money. Lawsuits aren't terribly effective if the defendant is indigent. Makes no sense for him to hide like this. Unless, of course, Heather is right and the guy's legit nuts. He might have a paranoid distrust of everything to do with the legal system. In trying to track this guy down, Tammy found a bunch of stuff on Desmond's Facebook page that makes me think he's one of those sovereign citizen types.

Unfortunately, he also seems to be quite patient. Or, perhaps, paranoid. An hour and seven minutes of sitting on the roof later, he still hasn't tried to leave. Desmond might be afraid I'm doing exactly what I'm doing and waiting for him, or he's convinced I believed Colby about him not being here and I gave up. Could also be that he feels he's 'safe' from me in someone else's house because I can't barge in without permission.

My phone rings. The Caller ID comes up as Boone, Benjamin. That's Milo's father. Since the call doesn't hit me with an inexplicable sense of doom, I have a feeling he isn't calling me to end my involvement in the case because the police found a body. The roof of an apartment building is a strange place to take calls, but lots of things about my life are strange.

"Samantha Moon," I say by way of answering.

"Hi," says a child. "You're the lady who came to our house."

"Saffron?" I ask.

"Yeah," says the girl, trying to be a little quiet.

"Is something wrong?"

"Uh huh. Milo's missing."

Ugh. I walked into that one, didn't I? "I know, sweetie. I'm trying to find him."

"I heard Milo talking a little while ago," half-whispers Saffron. "You said you wanted us to tell you if we heard anything, an' my parents put your number on the fridge."

Wow. Is it sad I'm impressed a nine-year-old knows how to old-school dial a phone number without going through a contacts page on a cell phone? Heh. Guess I'm becoming cynical in my 'old age.'

"Okay," I say. "But why are you whispering?"

"'Cause." She pauses as if looking over her shoulder. "My parents think I imagined hearin' him. But I swear I didn't make it up. *I swear.*"

I lean forward, instantly forgetting a man named Desmond Carter even exists. All my thoughts coalesce around the idea of *why* she might hear her brother's voice in the house. The first two explanations to hit me aren't the greatest, but they make the most sense. Maybe he's fully converted to a vampire, and he's hiding in the basement without his family's knowledge. Or... his ghost is back and trying to talk to them.

"Where did you hear him?" I ask. "And what did he say?"

"Umm... I was in my room and I heard Milo sort of calling for Mom or Dad, like he was trying to get them to come look at something."

I blink. Okay, that kind of shuts down the notion of a vampire boy who doesn't want to be found. Hate to say it, but a ghost roaming the house would be more likely to try and get his parents' attention. Damn. The problem is... I can't see ghosts anymore. Definitely not like I used to. And yeah, a haunting would be one explanation for the weird energy in the air.

For some reason, though, I still keep coming back to the idea Milo's gone vampire. A kid vampire who has no idea what happened to them can easily suffer a period of temporary craziness. That poor bastard Joseph Keeley certainly looked like he had a run-in with a frantic, and genuine, vampire. The second body, not so much. But… yeah, the first one was definitely a vampire.

Well, as definite as I can be.

Crap. If Milo is a vampire, he's going to need some mentoring. This would be right around the time he'd start to get hungry again after the feeding on the teacher. If he's in his house, his family could wind up on the menu when his sanity goes out the window. It all depends on if he knows what he's become and what his body wants.

I get myself worked up thinking about little Saffron innocently trying to hug her brother because she thinks he came home safe and ending up shredded because he lost control of himself. Takes me a moment to rein in my emotions so my voice sounds normal.

"All right. I'll be right there."

"You believe me?" asks Saffron.

"I do."

"Thanks," she says, a smile in her voice. "I'm not telling stories."

"I know, sweetie."

"Why don't my parents believe me?"

"Well, maybe something strange happened that grown-ups often have trouble coping with."

She gasps.

"Strange doesn't always mean bad. Just… strange. Things adults don't believe in anymore."

"Like magic?" asks the girl.

I exhale. No sense bringing up the 'v' word until I know for sure. "Yeah. Like magic."

Chapter Eleven
Imagination

The instant I leap through the dancing flame to the front yard of the Boone house, my phone rings again.

I lift it up, expecting the call to be from the parents, intending to apologize for Saffron 'bothering me' and telling me not to waste time dropping by. But it's not. It's Allison. I hastily answer.

"Hey, Allie."

"Sam… sorry it's taken me so long." She huffs. "Working from just a photo and a game controller is a challenge."

"Any chance you got something or are you just calling to tell me you haven't forgotten?" I ask.

"Well…" Allison emits a soft 'mmph' noise, which tells me she fell backward on her sofa. "I've been trying to distant see him or get any sort of psychic read possible, but there hasn't been much."

"Not much means you got *something,* right?"

"Yeah." She chuckles. "Dunno how useful it will be, though. I get cold. Like serious cold. Lots of snow. I'm almost certain he's really far away from here, but can't tell where. Whenever I focus on the picture, I pick up a lot of confusion, fear, homesickness. And, yeah, cold."

I furrow my brow. Cold could mean morgue, but... her thinking he's gone extremely far away? That's odd.

"Can you tell if he's still alive?" I ask.

"Yeah. I'm pretty sure he is. The fear isn't very extreme. It's more like 'I'm gonna get in so much trouble' type of fear."

"Huh. Odd."

"Ya think?" Allison laughs. "I'll keep trying to get more, but it might be futile without more of a connection, like if I had him on the phone."

I smirk. "If we had him on the phone, we could just ask him where he is."

"Oh. Right." She yawns. "I'm gonna grab a nap. Sorry I haven't been able to come up with anything more useful."

"It's all right." I gaze up at the clouds. "You mostly killed my worst fear about the case. Hope is definitely useful."

"Okay, good. Talk later."

We say goodbye and hang up. I gaze at the

house. Still, the place is infused with inexplicable energy. It's hardly the strongest paranormal charge I've ever felt anywhere, nor is it particularly gloomy. It's just... weird.

Okay, considering all the nothing Tammy and I —and the police—have been able to find about Milo's disappearance, it's time to start considering less rational explanations. Like… maybe faeries got him. Though, they don't usually steal children older than infants. My newfound hope Milo isn't a vampire changes my perception of the supernatural charge in the air. It's gone from scary to simply whacky.

I simultaneously step up onto the porch, put the phone back in my rear pocket, and ring the doorbell.

"I got it!" yells Saffron from somewhere inside the house.

A moment later, I'm greeted by a spritely blonde child in a pink dress and black leggings. The child seems thrilled to see me, but also like she's been crying recently.

"You look upset."

Saffron grinds her toe into the rug. "My big brother is missing and I'm sad."

Ben rushes over, giving me a surprised stare. "Ms. Moon? Did you find anything?"

"I'm still working on it. Following up on a lead."

Disappointment clouds his expression. "What sort of lead?"

"Saffron told me she heard him today."

He hangs his head. "Saf, we asked you not to pester her with nonsense. This is serious. Your brother is missing."

She starts to breathe rapidly, as if an explosion of tears is imminent.

"It's fine." I rest a hand on the girl's shoulder. "This case is really unusual, and I don't mean the sort of unusual to happen once every fifty years. I mean... well, this might sound a bit difficult to believe, but my instincts are telling me Milo might be experiencing something on the paranormal scale."

Ben's attention shifts from Saffron to me. "Are you serious? I thought my wife hired a private investigator, not a crackpot."

"I'm a PI but I also dabble in the crazy stuff too," I say, laying it out there. "Please give me a moment before you dismiss your daughter's experience."

He throws his hands up in frustration, but invites me inside anyway. We head to the kitchen, Saffron following us with her head down like she's still expecting to get in a heap of trouble. Fortunately, she's not crying yet.

"Coffee?" asks Ben.

"Sure. Thank you." I gaze around at the walls and ceiling, opening my senses for anything that wants to make itself known. "They say desperation often breeds strange beliefs."

"Exactly my point." Ben gestures the coffee pot

at his daughter. "She really wants her brother to be okay, so she's imagining she can still hear him."

"What if she didn't imagine it?" I ask.

Saffron's hazel eyes practically sparkle with adoration... or maybe hope.

"You can't be serious." Ben hands me a mug. "Cream or sugar?"

"Little of both, please. And I am. Very much so."

He nods, hands me a sugar pourer, then goes to the fridge for the milk.

Kaitlyn walks in carrying a basket of laundry. "We should—" She cuts her gaze from Ben to me. "Ms. Moon?"

"Saf called her," says Ben in a beleaguered tone.

"Oh, honey." Kaitlyn sighs. "You really shouldn't bother people with your stories."

"Not a story," says Saffron. "I really heard Milo."

Ben chuckles. "Seems you hired a psychic medium, too."

Kaitlyn raises an eyebrow. "Huh? What? Have you found something?"

"Not yet." I raise a 'slow down' hand. "Since you're all here now... let me ask. Do any of you get a strange feeling in this house?"

Saffron nods. Her parents appear oblivious.

"With my son missing," says Kaitlyn, "I've not been thinking much about anything else."

"We're not into that 'vibes' nonsense." Ben

frowns.

I nod at him. "Fair enough. The first time I was here, I noticed an unusual energy in the air permeating the house. Can't say it's bad or good, just odd. But it's definitely here. In most every case I've ever been involved with where a child has gone missing, there has been at least some tiny shred of evidence connected to the disappearance. A sighting, a piece of clothing found, a window left open where they snuck out... *something*. But, in Milo's case, it's like he simply disappeared."

The parents both stare at me.

"I've been to every bus stop, train station, and Uber office within fifty miles. No one's seen or heard from Milo. There are no signs of forced entry on the house, no signs of him sneaking out. His friends are unaware of him having any plans to try to get back to Ohio. There should have been something at this point to at least point me in a direction, but there's not."

Ben rubs his forehead. "Kids have gone missing without a trace before. Leaping to something paranormal is a bit too much of a stretch. Like that Bermuda Triangle nonsense."

"There has to be *some* evidence, right?" Kaitlyn hastily sets the laundry basket on the counter and proceeds to pace around.

Saffron stares up at her parents, trying to apologize with a stare.

"I told you that I'd exhaust everything possible

to find Milo. Even if that extends to the strange." I glance back and forth between the parents. "It doesn't bother me at all that your daughter called. Please don't be upset with her. This is not wasted time as far as I'm concerned. As implausible as it might be, I'd like to check every possibility."

The Boones exchange a glance, then give me a look like they think I'm nuts... but they really are desperate enough to see where this goes.

Since they aren't protesting, I shift my attention to the daughter. "Where were you when you heard him?"

"In my room." She points at the hallway. "He sounded like he was far away. Mom and Dad didn't hear him."

"Let me listen. I have good ears." I wink at her.

Saffron grins and scurries out of the kitchen.

The parents continue staring at me.

"Kids can be more sensitive to things like spirits," I say. "It *is* possible she heard something. Might not be Milo, but I need to check on it."

"Her brother's disappearance has really hit her hard," says Kaitlyn in a near-whisper. "We're thinking about therapy."

I exhale. "Well, if she needs help coping, it's not necessarily a bad idea. One moment."

They watch me walk down the hall after the girl. The faint supernatural tingle in the air gains strength the closer I get to the kids' bedrooms. It's still not overwhelming or even impressive.

"I was here." Saffron hops up to sit on her bed. "Like this, and I heard him out in the hall."

I stand beside the bed, gazing around in hopes of finding a particular direction the strange energy originates from. Alas, it's everywhere. Ben and Kaitlyn appear in the doorway after a moment. They stand there together, watching us and gradually shifting from hopeful to 'we're sorry she bothered you' in their expressions. Ben's also got a hint of 'next time you hire a PI, try not to get a kooky new age psychic weirdo.'

After almost five minutes of us all waiting in total silence, Ben says, "Sorry she bothered you."

"Mom?" calls a distant boyish voice. "Dad?"

Saffron perks up. "I heard him again!"

I raise a hand at the parents in a 'hold on a moment' gesture. "Milo?"

"Can you guys hear me?" The boy's voice sounds as if he's shouting from a football field away.

"I can hear you," I yell.

The parents flinch.

"It won't open," shouts Milo.

Ooh! I think he heard me. "Where are you?"

"I dunno!"

Saffron grabs my arm and hugs it. "That's him! That's Milo!"

The parents again exchange a glance. They clearly don't hear their son or they would be losing their minds. Instead, they look mournful, totally giving off a 'crap, our daughter's clinically insane' mood. Not waiting for them to do or say anything else, I gently push past them into the hallway.

"Milo, keep talking. Where are you?"

"I said I don't know," shouts the boy. "It's all snowy and stuff."

The sound of his voice draws my attention to a trapdoor in the ceiling—likely a fold-down attic stairway. I grab the cord and pull. Sure enough, the panel opens downward to reveal a collapsible ladder. A tangible wave of supernatural energy rolls over me like a dense gas spilling down from the attic above. Both parents stand there dumbfounded as I extend the ladder and make my way up.

"Keep talking, Milo," I yell.

"I'm here," says the boy—now louder.

Kaitlyn gasps/shrieks. "I heard him!"

Ben's making a face like he thinks he's just snapped and lost his mind.

Okay, so maybe this isn't spirit voices the child is sensitive to. She just has really keen hearing. Milo's voice isn't phantasmal, just extremely faint. Now that I've opened the attic hatch, it seems the parents can hear him, too. I climb up into the attic, surrounded by dozens of wooden trunks, cardboard boxes, plastic storage bins, and some older looking sheet-covered furniture. I don't know who in their right mind would bother lugging heavy objects up a rickety folding stairway. Good chance it was *not* the Boones. They haven't lived here long enough. All the sheet-covered items appear dusty as heck, definitely having been here undisturbed for a decade or more.

"Milo?" I call.

"I wanna go home," shouts the boy—his voice coming from the tallest sheet-covered object.

While I can't see what it is thanks to the linen, it's about seven feet high, thin, and three-ish feet wide. Based on shape alone, I'm tempted to say it's a freestanding mirror. Oh, shit. Mirrors are powerful when things get weird.

I move around a pile of blue plastic bins to a clearing in front of said mirror. On the floor in front of it is a shoebox-sized chest, open, and a bizarre metal implement that looks like something ancient sailors might have used to navigate with, like a sextant… only it's not. A long, bronze arc connects a handle to some globes. Two ruby spheres the size of cherry tomatoes sparkle with light that shouldn't be hitting them. It's also giving off a faint wisp of smoke. The bare wood floor has dark brown burn marks where the tool appears to have been dropped.

Bare footprints about the right size for a somewhat-small boy Milo's age disturb the dust in the area, the two closest to the mirror are smeared forward—like some powerful force vacuumed him into a portal.

I facepalm. Dammit.

Well, at least he's not a vampire.

I reach for the sheet...

Chapter Twelve
Elsewhere

And lift it out of the way.

Beneath it is indeed a freestanding tall mirror in an ornately carved wooden frame. Seeing an antique like this is odd enough. What's *odder* is the surface of said mirror is not showing me a reflection, rather a window into… elsewhere. A small Inuit type figure stands on the other side of the glass, shin deep in snow. They're wrapped in a parka like something you'd see in a documentary about ancient Siberian tribes. The clothing is definitely not from North Face.

Behind the bundled-up figure, miles and miles of snowy hills stretch toward not-too-distant mountain peaks. At least it looks like Earth. I haven't had the best luck with dimensions lately. No telling where this leads or who I'm looking at.

"Hello?"

"Who are you?" asks the miniature Sherpa—in Milo's voice.

"Milo?" I blink.

"Yeah." The boy reaches up and briefly exposes his face out from under a fur-lined covering. "It's me. Who are you?"

Oh wow, he really *is* small for his age. He looks closer to eleven than thirteen. I hold out a hand. "Can you walk through? I'll explain in a minute."

"No." He bangs a mitten-covered hand on the inside of the mirror. "It won't let me go back."

The snow seemingly comes to life behind him. It takes me a few seconds to mentally process what my eyes are telling me. It's not snow, but a huge, hairy, white ape-like creature—and it's looming up behind the boy, raising both fists like it's about to pound him into mush.

There are times when my overdeveloped motherly instincts get me in trouble. This is one of those times. Without thinking, I grab the nearest, most weapon-like object in sight—a hockey stick leaning against a trunk—and hurl myself at the monster. The instant my body passes through what *should* be solid glass, magical energy yeets me forward. Yes, I said yeet. I learned it from my kids. Aren't I a cool mom?

At least, I think I used 'yeet' correctly.

It's as if two big guys came out of nowhere behind me, scooped me off my feet, and threw me. Thanks to my supernatural reflexes, I manage to control the fling and channel it into a two-handed Red Sonja barbarian warrioress attack.

The hockey stick snaps over the monster's head with a *crack* that seems to echo for miles. I land on my feet in front of the thing—which now seems really damn large—clutching about four feet of stick. My attack appears to have momentarily stunned the creature, though it does not seem injured in the slightest bit, more perplexed.

I'm perplexed too. I have, of course, seen something similar... though in a wooded environment—and not covered in white fur. And certainly not in a murderous rage, though Kingsley might have something to say about that. Though these appear distant cousins of the hulking beasts I came across in the Pacific Northwest... they are nowhere near as intelligent. At least, I didn't think so. Of course, back then, I could communicate with them telepathically.

But that is a tale for another time.

Meanwhile, Milo picks himself up, rotates toward me, and lets out a startled yelp.

The creature pivots toward him.

"Get back!" I shout, while breaking the already broken stick into an even smaller piece over the monster's furry shoulder.

Ignoring me, it swats at the boy. Its hand is about the same size as Milo's entire torso. The kid leaps to the side, mostly avoiding a direct hit. The beast's walloping swing catches him in a grazing blow, launching him into the air. He spins head over feet three times before landing in the snow at least twenty yards away.

Growling, I jump in an effort to club the thing in the head again. The now-two-foot-long stick doesn't appear to bother the monster much. Its features, though seriously apelike, are human enough to project a dismissive 'what the heck are you trying to do' sort of quality in the side-eye squint it's giving me.

After regarding me for a second or two, it tries to backhand me out of the way so it can get to Milo. I duck the giant, white-furred arm, then whack it over the head a few more times until the remaining piece of hockey stick breaks again. The maybe twelve-inch fragment left in my grasp isn't any use as a weapon—not that the whole stick proved much better—so I toss it aside.

Milo gasps for air.

"Are you okay?" I yell.

"I think so," rasps the boy. "Coat's really thick."

Great. I had to go and return Excalibur. How crazy is my life that *not* carrying a sword around ends up being a serious problem? I almost reflexively reach for Azrael's sword, but stop myself. It's not there anymore, either. I had to step down to protect my family. A job like that is fit for immortals with nothing to lose, no family, no attachments. Demons will exploit anything they can to win, including loved ones.

C'mon, Sam. You can handle a giant snow monkey without a magical sword. It's just a… what do they call these things? Yeti, I think. Well, whatever he is, he's huge, furry, and smells like a wet dog. He also wants to pummel a presumably innocent boy into meat paste. I have serious objections to that.

So much for my hockey offense. Then again, I didn't really play sports in school. Time for a different tactic. The next time the yeti attempts to punch me, I weave around its massive fist and hammer my knuckles into its face using all my strength. Safe to say, we have left normality behind. I don't care if this thing realizes I'm way stronger than a mortal woman should be. What's it going to do? Call the CIA on me? Sell its story to the National Enquirer?

The hit knocks the yeti into a backward lean. Judging by how wide his eyes are now, I'm going to guess he's coming to the realization I'm an actual problem he'll need to deal with rather than dismiss. He emits a seriously loud, angry bellowing roar. Haven't heard a noise like that since I worked at HUD and the Dallas Cowboys won in a shutout against... I want to say Green Bay? I don't really pay much attention to sports. Haven't thought about it in years.

Yeah, though. This thing sounds like a man who just lost six grand on a football bet while simultaneously watching a team he despises kick the snot out of his favorite team. Okay, to be fair, this yeti *is* eight feet tall. He's probably a bit louder.

"Run!" yells Milo.

Sure, and let this thing grab you? No way, kiddo.

Enraged, the yeti raises both massive hands over his head and tries to *Donkey Kong* me to China. As in, drive me like a nail through the entire planet to the other side. Fortunately for me, he's not the fastest critter. Poor thing puts so much power into the smash, he falls flat on his face when I dodge.

127

Before he can get up, I swoop in and punch him in the side of the head in a rapid flurry of blows. Spittle, ice crystals, and maybe a tooth or two go flying.

It flails, giving a fearful sort of cry. Being so close to it, there's no chance for me to move out of the way. Thankfully, though, the proximity changes a smashing swing to a shoving one. I land on my back well out of its reach. Snow makes it somewhat challenging to get upright again fast. By the time I am on my feet again, the yeti is hoofing it into the snowy hills, evidently having had enough of little ol' me.

My knuckles ache like hell. Maybe I broke a finger or two. Yeah… probably not a great idea to punch a creature with a skull as thick as a door.

"Whoa…" Milo trudges over to me. "That was… awesome."

I look him over. Aside from a dusting of snow, he seems unhurt. The parka absorbed most of the force of the creature hitting him. Like me, it only seemed to have thrown him. "You hurt?"

"Nope. You?"

I wave my hand back and forth. "Nothing I won't get over in a few minutes."

Milo slouches. "Ugh. Now you're stuck here, too."

His words bring me back to the reality of our situation. I look past him at a door-sized hole in reality, looking into the attic of his house. Saffron and her parents peer at us through the opening.

"Do not touch the glass!" I yell. "You'll get pulled in, too."

Ben stares slack-jawed. If the look on his face is any indication, he'll likely not be able to speak for a few hours. Saffron appears thrilled to bits to see Milo is okay, and is completely ignoring the bizarreness of them having a portal in their attic. Kaitlyn shudders, evidently fighting the urge to reach through the glass.

The coldness here is a shock. If I'd been a normal mortal, I'd likely be freaking out right about now. It's brisk, for sure. This is the kind of cold that could freeze eyeballs and turn a man's beard into an ice sculpture in an hour. Milo had been barefoot and probably in pajamas. He clearly didn't bring the parka, the fur-stuffed leggings, or the thick boots with him, so there must be people here who found him before he froze to death.

Good sign. Wherever 'here' is, the locals are reasonably nice.

I look back at the portal to say something reassuring about getting him home soon—only to stare in helpless bafflement as the opening fades away.

"You better go inside before you freeze," says Milo.

"Inside?" I glance around at endless snow in every direction except for a vast-looking pine forest (also snowy) to my right. "There's no 'inside' here."

Milo points in the opposite direction from the

woods. "Over there. A whole village."

Well, that does explain the parka. "Fine. Lead the way."

Chapter Thirteen
Definitely Something Supernatural

I soon find myself on the outskirts of a village high up in the mountains.

A few dozen people, all wearing similar sorts of parkas and big furs pause in their activities to take note of my presence. They are probably confused to see me standing here so casually despite being woefully underdressed for this weather.

It's good to be supernatural.

Okay, I might as well get the obvious stupidity out of the way first. I fish out my phone and check it. Shocker: no signal. Let's see what sort of bizarre error the GPS app throws when someone attempts to use it in an alternate dimension.

I have to tap the screen twice for it to register my fingertip. The app opens and gives me this 'searching for satellite' message. Yeah, guessing it's going to be a while. Much to my surprise, however, it gets a connection. The map zooms to one side.

According to my phone, I'm in Nepal, a few miles westish of a point of interest called Singu Chuli.

The average person getting flung through a hole in space to land halfway around the world would be freaked the heck out. Me? I'm relieved. Still Earth. Still normal world. No problem. This certainly fits Allison's information: cold and far away.

Milo takes my hand. "C'mon. You're gonna freeze."

I walk with him into the village. People regard us, their expressions—as much as I can see past face coverings—curious. A few attempt to speak, though none try using English. As best I can, I smile and wave, attempting to convey friendliness. A few villagers hurry off. They don't seem alarmed. Going to guess they're off to grab extra warm clothing for me the way they did for Milo.

He pulls me into a hut. It's a single, round room with a fire pit in the middle. A hole at the top of the animal-hide shelter lets the smoke out and a little sunlight in. It's reasonably warm inside, enough for the woman and teenage girl who happen to be here already not to need full parkas. They both try speaking to us, though soon resort to mostly gestures and pantomime to communicate. I *think* Milo manages to explain to them I showed up the same way he did, but it's anyone's guess really what they're thinking.

They do smile at me and offer me a cup of hot something. I think it's tea. They must think I'm frozen or on the way to it. I humor them and do my best to consume the odd flavor without grimacing.

Milo shrugs off his upper parka to reveal a pajama shirt. Poor kid is even smaller than I imagined and scrawny like his sister. "Sorry, Miss."

"For what?"

"Being dumb."

"How were you dumb?" I ask.

"Playing with stuff in the attic." He fidgets. "I found this thing in a box and it lit up. Thought it was a toy, but it didn't seem to have a switch or batteries. While I was fiddling with it trying to figure out where the batteries went, it made a flash and something pulled me real hard. I landed in the snow."

"You had no way to know it would do anything." I nudge him on the arm. "Who would believe people could open mirrors like doorways."

He whistles. "Yeah, really. Are we in like Narnia or something?"

"No. This is Nepal." I glance at my phone. "Provided this thing isn't going crazy and confused by interdimensional energies."

"Inter-what?"

"Never mind. Not sure I know what it means,

either."

Milo sighs. "The stupid portal thing closed behind me and I couldn't get home. The people here are nice, but I can't understand them. They keep drawing me pictures of snow monsters, like they think I can do something."

I finish off the tea, smile at the younger of the two women, and offer her the cup back. She takes it, gives me a once over, then nods approvingly. Her non-reaction to my modern clothing helps convince me my phone is correct. We probably are still in the real world, merely a highly remote part of it.

"Are my parents mad at me?" asks Milo.

"No. They think you were kidnapped." I exhale. "Pretty sure they're not going to handle the truth very well, but… I can say with a reasonable degree of confidence, they won't be angry with you."

"Whew." He pantomimes wiping sweat from his forehead. "I don't know how to get home from here, or even explain to the people I need to go home. I think we're really out in the middle of nowhere."

"Yeah." I glance at the phone screen. "You can say that. Way up in the mountains, too."

"Maybe it's the winter season or something and the roads are too snowy." He shrugs.

I chuckle. "There aren't any roads out here, kid. Pretty sure our options are limited to walking, riding a horse, or taking a helicopter. Horse might not even be doable here."

"Oh." He glances down. "Do you have a

horse?"

"Nope."

"Helicopter?"

"Not exactly."

Milo reaches for the parka. "Are we gonna walk, then?"

"Nope."

He looks up at me. "We're staying? But I gotta go home."

The older of the two women, who's probably in her early forties, holds up a ratty piece of paper, almost a scroll. It's got a drawing of a yeti on it, surrounded by fancy calligraphic writing. It looks similar to Japanese kanji, but clearly is not. She taps the drawing, gestures at Milo, then me, tilting her head inquisitively.

"I saw one. It tried to attack Milo," I say, despite having no hope she'll understand me.

"They don't speak English." The boy shrugs. "But they're super nice to me. This family lets me sleep here, and they gave me warm clothes."

"That's great of them." I smile at the two women. "Wish I could communicate, but… c'mon. Gonna take you home now."

He squints. "Uhh, really? Aren't we going to need to like pack up a bunch of food? Get a sled with dogs or something?"

"Nah. Trust me." I wink and take his hand. "You'll be home soon."

Milo doesn't protest, but he's giving me almost

the same look his father did when I started talking about paranormal explanations for his disappearance.

In almost any other circumstance, I'd take him somewhere out of sight so no one witnesses us teleporting away. However, it's freakin' cold out there. Also, we're in a super remote tribal village in Nepal. If they tell anyone an American appeared out of nowhere and promptly disappeared back into thin air, most would laugh the story off as the product of vivid imaginations or local legends.

Sort of like how modern society doesn't take the Native American stories of skinwalkers seriously.

I close my eyes and concentrate on the dancing flame, envisioning Milo's bedroom.

Just as the tiny candle flame appears in the blackness, a distant woman emits a terrified scream. It's the sort of scream one might expect to hear from someone about to be chopped into pieces by the monster in a cheesy horror movie.

"Yati!" shouts both women in here. "Yati yahām̐ cha!"

"I think she said the yeti is here," whispers Milo.

Another eight seconds of concentration and we should be safe back in California. But... I have an overdeveloped conscience. It's totally not in me to bail out and leave these villagers to get pummeled by snow apes.

The same woman shrieks again.

"One sec, kiddo." I let go of his hand, get up, and start for the door. "You stay inside."

Grr. Find the kid and go home. Sure.

Nothing is ever so easy, is it?

Chapter Fourteen
A Hairy Situation

Against the apparent protests of the two women who live in this hut, I run outside.

The scene unfolding around me is chaotic and surreal. At least eight yetis are attacking the village, having mostly come from the north. Multiple villagers are attempting to fend them off with spears. Other people run around in a mad dash for cover or to collect children. Despite me finding myself in the midst of a freakin' *yeti* attack, the strangest part isn't the big furry creatures.

It's a woman.

She stands out from the locals due to her not wearing a heavy parka. No, she's wearing this crazy airy pixie dress like something you might see on a forest elf. She's also blue. Like almost Smurf blue.

Hair-like strands of silvery white icicles cascade behind her as she whirls around a yeti, savaging it with a pair of crystalline swords.

It's now my turn to make the 'you gotta be kidding me' face. All the things I've seen in my life, watching a blue-skinned woman fight yetis in a remote Nepalese village shouldn't leave me stunned and staring. Maybe part of my brain still tries to cling to at least an imaginary version of sanity instead of this high fantasy movie my life loves to keep turning into. Of course, all those creatures of folklore had to be inspired by something, right? Maybe people ages ago saw them for real and for reasons known only to the creatures, they became more and more scarce until humanity regarded them as myths.

The woman I heard scream before emits a third cry. The sound draws my attention to a parka-clad villager sprinting away from a bounding yeti. I get the feeling the woman had been attempting to elude it by ducking around huts… but it finally saw her.

Violence isn't often my first resort. However, these creatures appear to be simple-brained monsters intent on murder, not any sort of civilized society. Certainly not the highly evolved Sasquatch I'd recently come across. Indeed, these snow giants have also apparently killed a handful of villagers already—or at least injured them enough to lie where they fell.

I race for the one chasing the woman, pausing

briefly to grab a spear from a fallen male villager. The yeti doesn't have a chance to react to my attack as it's way too slow. It barely raises an arm in an effort to defend itself as I plunge the spear into the creature's side. Not going to try for a head shot. Sure, the brain is a guaranteed kill, but my faith in these rickety spears is only slightly stronger than my faith in the old hockey stick.

Two feet of spear sink into its furry hide. Surprisingly little blood comes out of the wound. With a gurgle, the yeti's charge collapses into a stumbling fall. It crashes to the ground, throwing up a blinding spray of sparkling snow as it slides to a stop. The screaming villager continues running, either oblivious to or not caring I killed the thing chasing her.

I hurry over and grab the spear, expecting to break it off rather than pull it out. Shockingly, the instant I tug on the weapon, the yeti corpse dematerializes into a low-hanging cloud of dense cyan smoke.

What in the hell...?

There's no blood on the spear, either.

Illusions? No... can't be. It was solid. Five or six potentially dead villagers make a strong case for them *not* being illusions. Maybe golems of some kind. As in, not really alive. Works for me. Zero guilt killing something that doesn't really exist. My confidence in the spear increases. I zoom back into the fray, coming at the yetis from their right flank.

The blue woman is a veritable dervish, engaging four at once. They aren't fast enough to hit her, but her rapid and shallow counterattacks mostly annoy them. It's as if she's only trying to keep their attention off the villagers.

The yeti's pronounced slowness is the only reason mortal humans have any chance whatsoever facing them. Strange, I don't remember the Sasquatch moving this slow. In fact, when fighting Kingsley, they were downright fast.

Anyway, an ordinary guy fighting one of these snow monsters probably feels like a traditional vampire preying on a human, accelerating themselves to the point it's beyond easy. In my case, it's about as challenging as stabbing mannequins. They are, however, incredibly strong. Grazing blows throw men and women dozens of feet into the air. Any solid hit is pretty much instant death for mortals. Six-inch-thick parkas can do only so much when you get hit by a wrecking ball.

I kill three in a row while fighting my way in from the side. The yetis all burst into smoke within six seconds of death. Some of the locals get kills as well, their yetis doing the same. Every so often, the blue-skinned woman decides to thrust rather than slash and takes one out.

It's about to seem like we have the upper hand when grunting to my left makes me look… and I wish I hadn't.

More yetis—well more than a hundred—are

barreling across the snowy hills toward the village. They're still at least a mile away, but that many... even I'd get overwhelmed. Come on, Sam. Think. What the hell can I do to stop a literal army of ice monkeys? Actually, they're closer to Neanderthal than ape.

Ice. Hmm. Fire maybe?

Where the heck am I going to get enough fire to scare off a hundred yetis?

Perhaps I can be of some assistance, says Talos in the back of my mind.

I eye the village. They're quite busy at the moment and not paying any attention to me. Oh, hell. Not like anyone would ever believe them. Besides, a single dragon is no less strange than an army of ape monsters.

Fire! That's right!

After dashing behind the nearest hut, I strip out of my clothes. Haven't gone from zero to naked this fast since my college days. Hey, girls can be wild, too. As far as the extreme cold here goes, my T-shirt and jeans don't make much difference compared to being nude. The only thing keeping me functional is my ability to heal. Continually having frostbite and healing it probably should hurt like hell, but my brain is simply disregarding the ouch.

I'm bare-assed for only a few seconds before Talos leaps forward out of my subconscious. To my perspective, the hut shrinks to the size of a large easy chair. The shadow of my dragon form falls over it. His inner heat is awesome. Hey, I'm from Cali. We don't do cold.

With a heavy *whumpf* of leathery wings, I launch myself into the air. Pretty sure a black dragon stands out fairly obviously in an environment like this where everything is blindingly white. Snow covered ground, snow-dusted huts, snowy pine forest in the distance. Even the sky is kind of a pale whitish grey at the moment.

What they say about people having a tendency not to look up apparently holds true for yetis as well. They don't appear to notice me approaching from the air.

It has been some time since you have done this, says Talos' voice in my head. *Do you remember how?*

I do, yes. I think.

I had, in fact, used it to great effect when battling Lichtenstein in the middle of Lake Elsinore. Of course, Lichtenstein had been a giant worm at the time. But yeah, I didn't go around breathing fire willy-nilly. It's a great way to burn down the state of California.

You were an old pro at this stuff, once.

Right… multiple reincarnated souls ago when I was a dragon.

I veer around in a curving path to fly east-to-west over the yetis. They're storming toward the village in a pack that's more line than group, though it's hardly organized. As I start to think about exhaling a flamethrower, a tingle spreads around the inside of my chest, slightly above where the stomach should be. Now's not the time for me to ponder the mechanics of dragon flame. Dunno if I have a special 'gall bladder' full of oil that bursts into fire as soon as it hits air or if this is pure magic.

Also, don't care… as long as it works.

For no particular reason, I wait until it feels like I'm at the right distance. Old instincts or whatever coming back, perhaps. As soon as it seems proper to do so, I open my enormous mouth and attempt to unleash the fires of hell.

My first try in a long time produces a blob of flaming lava snot. The globule of sticky magical napalm is about the size of a Prius. It splatters into the ground, covering at least four yeti, then bursts into a shower of a thousand smaller blobs. Nothing remains of the creatures who sustained a direct hit. They presumably disintegrated to smoke on contact. Other yeti who aren't instantly destroyed begin running around on fire and screaming.

You rather choked on that one, Sam. Deep breath. Release it smoothly.

Right. I remember now.

I wing around for another strafing pass. This time, I think Zen thoughts. Deep breath in, deep breath out—and *woooooosh.*

Mama has a flamethrower.

I've produced a fifty-foot-long streamer of dark crimson flames that's burned a trench through the snow at least twice that length and caught probably fourteen yetis in its path. Again, I swerve around. This time I'm fully confident and know exactly what it feels like. My third gout of flame is epic. The roar of the burn, the feeling of power, the heat… glorious.

Only problem is I'm incinerating empty ground.

The yetis are hauling ass for the forest. They've totally broken whatever semblance of 'ranks' they had and have surrendered to almost blind panic. Not a trace of yeti gore remains anywhere in sight, confirming these things aren't real. Or… they're quasi-real. Genuine enough to exist and cause damage, but transient to the point they return from whence they came if killed.

They are conjurations, Sam.

What? I blink. Conjurations? That sounds like magic.

It is. Something is summoning them into being. For all intents and purposes, they are real… until they are killed.

Wait, so someone is literally making these snow apes?

Essentially. They are not apes. As you pointed out earlier, they are their own species. Yetis.

Are actual yetis a thing?

Yes. However, these are not genuine yetis, but copies. The real ones do not exist in such large numbers so close together. Also, they would avoid humans, not raid their villages. They are closer in makeup to the Sasquatch you have become familiar with.

Don't suppose you have any idea why this is happening?

I do not, alas. Perhaps the nymph will be able to offer that information.

Nymph? Oh, the blue woman. She's a nymph?

Correct. A frost nymph, to be specific.

Great. Just when things can't get any crazier. What do I need to know about frost nymphs?

They are benevolent. She is likely a protector of the natural order.

Okay. Sounds good. Darn.

What is wrong?

The yetis are retreating.

Is that not a good thing, Sam?

It is, but it also means I need to go back to my usual form. You are so warm.

He smiles mentally at me.

No sense making this take forever. I could wait and enjoy being warm for a while, but I'll inevitably have to go back. Also, I need to get Milo home. Warmth can wait for California. Determined, I dive low to the ground and cruise back to the village, trying to weave among the snowdrifts to stay out of sight. When I get close enough to where it's near impossible for me to stay hidden, I reluctantly shift back into my normal form still in midair... then wing glide the last hundred yards or so and streak over to my clothes.

After hurrying back into my outfit, I walk around the hut and try to be casual.

Villagers are mostly cheering their victory over the yetis, though a few are staring skyward as if they definitely saw my Talos form. Whoops. Got seen. Meh. Whatever. Like I said, who will believe them? Hopefully, they won't associate me with the big black thing in the air. And hey, there are yetis rampaging around the hills here.

Who's going to care about a little ol' dragon?

Chapter Fifteen
Prophecies and So Forth

Did I mention there's a frost nymph?

Nimue, the Lady of the Lake, mentioned something about me running into one. Guess this is that moment. Said frost nymph is standing among the villagers, who don't really show much of any odd reaction to her presence. She spots me, smiles, and starts walking over. The woman is about my height, slender, and somewhat elven in appearance except for having rounded ears. Up close, a frosted sheen glimmers on her skin. Good chance the faint aura of blue light around her is her radiating coldness, but it's so damn frigid here I can't feel it compared to the environment.

"You are not mortal," says the nymph in a melodic, pretty voice laced with an almost bell-like quality—as if someone recorded her dialogue while wind chimes played in the background.

"What gave it away?" I deadpan. "Me traipsing about in a t-shirt, the wings, or the giant dragon?"

She emits a bright giggle. "All of the above, as humans say. I have been expecting you."

"Not exactly how I expected this meeting to go down."

"Indeed. You speak of your efforts to find the missing boy."

I nod. "Yeah. Crazy coincidence."

A nearby villager calls out in Nepali. The nymph responds. Whatever she said appears to make him quite happy as he proceeds to cheer and say something to the others, which gets them all cheering at me. Uh oh. What have I just been volunteered for?

"This has something to do with Milo?" I raise an eyebrow.

"Not directly." She shakes her head. "These villagers believe the boy is a hero foretold in the stories of their elders. The tales speak of the yeti abandoning their peaceful ways and becoming a menace, and of a foreigner arriving mysteriously one day. When this boy appeared here without explanation, they all believed him to be the one who would protect them from the yetis."

Be strong, Sam. Do not facepalm in front of the nice frost nymph.

"They seriously expected *Milo* to fight off the

yetis?" I blink. "Have you seen him? He's… small."

She smiles. "I do not believe he is the one foretold to end the yeti threat. That is you."

"I'm only here because of him."

"And yet you are a foreigner who appeared mysteriously." She raises an icy eyebrow as if to say 'gotcha.'

"True. It's obviously not the kid. But I don't really believe in prophecies."

"You don't?" She giggles again. "An immortal who pretends the supernatural is not real?"

"No…" I rub the bridge of my nose. "I mean… sure, prophecies can be a thing. I just don't think I'm important enough to be the subject of one."

She brushes a cold hand over my cheek. "Not every prophecy is about saving all the world. Some of them are merely sparing one village from destruction. A mortal human is stirring up dark energies here that could threaten the surrounding areas as well. If he is successful, many will die."

"I thought you said this wasn't a 'save the world' type prophecy."

"It isn't." She smiles. "Merely a large portion of it. Not the *entire* world."

"Ugh."

Her smile fades to a look of concern. "He is not the main threat. When mortal society becomes aware of him and what he is doing, when their veil of ignorance shatters and they see the world for what it really is, they will react with great force to destroy him. You refer to such force as…" She cringes. "Nuclear weapons."

I stare at her for a moment. "You think world governments will react to a bunch of angry yetis with nukes?"

The nymph's expression goes stern. "They will react to the destruction of their reality, their false belief that things like yetis and magic are not real in the way that humans always react to that which they cannot control or understand."

Damn. She has a point. People lose their minds if the wrong celebrity gets eliminated from *Dancing With The Stars*. Prove magic is real to the global population? Sure. Yeah. They'd nuke something. Superpowers would either try to claim it for themselves or destroy the hell out of it before the other side got their hands on it. In short, it would be a giant mess… like the most chaotic episode of *Jerry Springer* ever.

Hmm. Now I wonder. Maybe some ancient elder spirits foresaw humanity devolving into such a lowly state that reality TV became a thing and we can't be trusted with magic anymore. The Kardashians could be why all the supernatural stuff went into hiding.

"All right. Fine. This is a bit outside the scope of private investigation." I make a pinchy gesture. "Just a bit."

"My kind are duty bound to keep the balance." She gives me a pleading look. "I am afraid too many of us have been killed. We are losing this fight here. Please. Help us."

I gesture at Milo, who's wandered over to eavesdrop on our conversation. "I need to take him home first. Then, I'll come back to see what I can do here."

She winces. "I do not think we have the time for you to travel so far."

"Don't worry." I wave Milo over and grin at her. "This will just take a moment."

Chapter Sixteen
Plausibility

Frustration and impatience are two things capable of making a person reckless.

Old age can, too... but that depends on the individual. Some oldsters get more cautious. Some surrender to wild abandon. Not that I'm old, but I've been around long enough to reach a point where what people think about me doesn't matter so much anymore. And sure, most people apply that logic to beauty or decorum—like the old lady running around in a Guns N' Roses T-shirt—not supernatural oddities.

Anyway, I'm standing in the middle of a village that just suffered a yeti attack while talking to a frost nymph. Something tells me if I teleport in front of people, they're not going to care. My urge to get this kid home is much stronger than my need to keep the supernatural on the down low. Things have already gone off the leash, so to speak.

With a firm grip on Milo's hand, I close my eyes and call the dancing flame. Within it, I picture the boy's bedroom. Might as well spare ourselves the climb down the rickety ladder, right? Wouldn't want the kid losing his balance in all those heavy furs and breaking his neck or something stupid right as we get him home.

The flame expands from the size of a candle to a doorway. I step through in my mind, pulling Milo with me.

"Whoa!" gasps the boy. "Holy shi—cow!"

I open my eyes to the sight of the kid's still-mostly-unpacked bedroom. "Nice save."

"Uhh, sorry." Milo begins opening his coat. "I'm not supposed to swear. My parents get upset."

"No worries. I think they'd let that one slide. Not every day you get to teleport."

He flings the massive parka off and drops it on the rug, then stares at me. His fur-lined leggings are so damn thick compared to his upper body they make him look like one of those Russian stacking dolls. "We just…"

"Yeah. We did. But…" I hold up a finger. "Most people can't handle stuff like this being real. It would be best if you didn't go around talking about teleportation, yetis, and so on. At best, it'll get you teased. At worst, probably sent to see a psychiatrist."

"Ack. Umm… what about my parents?" He slips off the heavy fur-lined leggings, revealing thin pajama pants covered in some manner of anime characters.

Merely looking at him standing there in PJs makes me shiver at the thought he got stranded high in the Nepalese mountains with such light clothing on. "Oh, yeah. Sure. Tell them the truth, but they might not be able to handle it either."

Meanwhile, the murmuring voices of Ben, Kaitlin, and Saffron filter down through the ceiling. Sounds like they're still in the attic trying to figure out how to 'turn the mirror' on again. Based on their conversation, my guess is the thing has reverted to being a normal reflective surface at the moment.

"Mom! Dad!" shouts Milo on his way out into the hall. He stops short at the sight of the attic ladder extended. "You guys up there?"

"Milo!" screams Saffron.

The tone of her voice, the excitement-slash-desperation, knowing she's nine, and having had kids that age myself, I brace for disaster and zoom into the corridor. Sure enough, Saffron attempts to run down the rickety attic ladder and ends up taking a tumble. Thankfully, my supernatural reflexes are good for more than just fighting demons and chasing down werewolves. I catch her before she can smack her head into the floor. In a smooth motion, I spin her upright and set her on her feet within hugging range of her brother.

Her enthusiasm momentarily stalls at confusion, as if she isn't exactly sure if she fell or not. It lasts only a few seconds before she's bouncing, cheering, and clamping onto Milo. Ben and Kaitlyn negotiate the ladder with much greater care. Soon, the whole family is squeezing together in an emotional clump. I quietly collapse the attic stairs and close the trapdoor.

After maybe ten minutes, things calm down enough for actual speaking. Milo begins apologizing for messing with the mirror and getting himself stranded. His parents tell him they don't think he did it on purpose, even though they sound like they're still having trouble believing what happened. This leads into them asking me to explain what happened.

For now, I leave out the yeti thing. There's only so much WTF normal people can handle in one dose.

"I'm not an expert on crazy magical artifacts or anything." I gesture at the ceiling. "However, it seems you have an enchanted mirror in your attic. Or, maybe that sextant looking thing is responsible and the mirror only happened to be a convenient reflective surface."

The parents stare at me.

"What do you mean?" asks Ben.

"You saw the metal thing with the ruby orbs on

it, right?"

He nods.

"That thing could be the problem, not the mirror. Milo was playing with it and it's possible it did something to the mirror, and could do a similar thing to *any* mirror. It's also possible the two items are connected." I offer a helpless shrug. "It's also possible that device is entirely nothing and the mirror did it all. Like I said, I don't do magic."

"You teleported," whispers Milo.

"Okay." I hold up a finger. "Fair point. I don't do lots of magic. Just a few things."

"Teleported?" Kaitlyn shifts her gaze from me to Milo and back again. "I'm not sure I understand."

"Like on Star Trek, Mom," says Milo. "One minute, we're in Nepal. The next, my room."

"Oof." Ben wipes a hand down his face. "I'd say I can't believe that but... here you are. I... don't really care so much what happened as long as you're safe."

"Sorry, Dad." Milo hugs his father.

"Stop apologizing already." Ben grins. "Okay, wow. We're going to have to come up with some way to explain this to the police."

Kaitlyn bites her lip. "Will we get in trouble if we say he just got lost?"

"I don't know." Ben shifts his jaw side to side. "We can't make up a fake kidnapping story because the police will keep investigating and wasting time."

"No, we can't." Kaitlyn folds her arms. "But we also can't tell them he got transported into a mirror. They'll lock us all up."

Milo emits a sigh. "I can say I tried to go home to Ohio, but chickened out and came home. Even if it gets me in trouble."

I raise an eyebrow. "Might get you sent to a therapist, but I doubt you'd get in legal trouble for it."

"Mom? Dad?" asks Saffron. "Why do we have a magic mirror in the attic? Is it gonna eat Milo again?"

"Good question." I peer up. "Where it came from, that is. I don't expect it will 'eat' anyone unless they mess around with it."

"And to be clear," says Ben, looking from his wife to me, "we're all comfortable using the term 'magic mirror'?"

I nod happily.

Kaitlyn shrugs. "It must've been Dad's. This house belonged to my parents. My mother passed recently. My father died four years ago. He was kind of unusual."

"I believe the term you're looking for is 'strange and eccentric,'" Ben chuckles. "In a good way, though. The man was nice enough, just off in his own little world."

Kaitlyn gives Ben side eye. "Doesn't seem like he was quite so crazy anymore, does it? If this stuff is real."

Most of the color drains from his face. "Uhh… yeah, wow."

"My mother knew something was off with the mirror." Kaitlyn fidgets. "She wanted to get rid of it and some other stuff he kept up there, but getting rid of it required touching it and it scared her."

"So what do we tell people?" asks Ben.

Kaitlyn flaps her arms. "We sure as heck don't tell anyone about magic mirrors, or Nepal, or tele-porting."

"Good plan," I say.

Ben raises an eyebrow. "We could go with the Ohio story for now. And maybe after seeing how much Milo missed home, it convinces us to sell this place and go back."

Both kids gasp in awe.

"Really?" Kaitlyn blinks. "But you just got that job."

"Yeah, but I could get my old one back."

"This house, though… you were so sick of that tiny apartment." Kaitlyn gazes around.

"For what we could sell this place for, we could buy a house twice its size in Ohio." Ben wags his eyebrows. "And you spent a week telling me how creepy this place was before we decided to move."

Kaitlyn shrugs. "It's something to talk about. I dunno... the place is growing on me a little. Maybe there's more secrets to discover."

"Well, if you do, you have my card," I say, and wink.

The kids stare at their parents much the same as if a Disneyland vacation were being talked about openly in front of them. Wow, they really do miss Ohio. Likely, they miss their friends more than anything. Moving is rough on kids.

Then again, moving into a house full of magic, all left over from their mystical grandfather, could be an adventure in and of itself. Heck it already was.

Anyway… my work here is done. Thankfully, Milo Boone is *not* a vampire. Not only is he still alive, his mouth is too small to have made those fang marks. I leave the family to enjoy their reunion and work out the particulars of how they're going to explain things to the police. This is one of those times where I just sort of forget the whole 'being paid' thing. The family isn't exactly in the best financial situation. I'm comfortable enough at the moment to let some cases go pro bono.

Call me a softie.

Chapter Seventeen
Triage

I should probably be more careful.

The number of people in the world who know I have unexplainable abilities just increased by four... plus, however many people live in that Nepalese village. Though, it's seriously unlikely any of those villagers will ever end up working the talk show circuit to speak about the strange foreigner with magical abilities. I mostly trust the Boone family won't sell me out, too. Some stories just aren't believable to the general public.

Of course, if the detectives working on Milo's missing person case are any good, it won't take them too long to develop doubts about any fabricated explanation for his disappearance. At least the family has it going for them that the truth is considered impossible by most people.

Speaking of impossible... seems I have a yeti issue to deal with. I'm half tempted to try to find a real sword before going back there. Got a feeling it's going to take more than an old hockey stick to deal with this problem.

Suppose I could simply rain fiery death on them from above again... but I'd prefer not to kill this man. At least, not unless I'm forced to. Those fake yetis are one thing—not really alive—but an actual human is a bit different.

In the back of my mind, I can almost hear Fang chuckling at me for being a weird vampire. He thinks it's strange for a vampire to be squeamish about killing mere mortals—even though he doesn't go around doing it himself... unless he, too, wants to incur the wrath of vampire hunters. Trust me, none of us do. Anyway, to him, it's like a vegan being upset over the killing of chickens or cows. I like the guy as a friend, but there's a reason we'd never work romantically.

So, I've got a guy using magic to summon ice apes to deal with. Seems like it shouldn't be too big a deal. It's not my normal preference, but a guy willing to destroy a village full of innocent people is not likely to be open to changing his mind from a simple conversation. This is undoubtedly going to take slapping him around a little first. Again, not my MO but, people *are* dead because of this guy. Getting a little rough with him won't bother me. It's sort of like the cop missing on purpose when trying to stuff a child abuser into the car and 'accidentally' ramming his head into the window.

I picture myself swooping down out of the air, tackling the guy, swinging him around to put his back against a tree and threatening him into compliance. Oh, who am I kidding? This guy killed villagers on a mad quest for power. He's probably not going to be intimidated easily, and even if he appears to surrender, he'd be lying.

Okay, Sam. Prepare.

There's a really good chance this man is going to need to die by my hand. If letting him live means innocent people die, I'll deal with the guilt. And hey, who knows? Maybe the nymph will have more information. Going to plan to keep looking for a non-fatal solution here.

Just as I close my eyes to begin the process of teleporting back to the village, my phone rings.

I swear, the Universe has one heck of a sense of timing.

Tammy's name is on the screen, so I don't hesitate to answer. "Hey, Tam Tam. What's up?"

"Hey, Ma. Was your phone off or something? Sherbet called the office since you weren't picking up the cell."

"I may have been *slightly* outside the coverage area not long ago…"

She pauses. "Did you go to another dimension again?"

163

"No, just Nepal."

"Oh. Well, Sherbet wants you to call him ASAP. He said there's another body."

Damn. That's awful soon. Most serial killers space things out a bit more. Wait. Stop assuming. Just because Milo isn't a new vampire doesn't mean there isn't one out there. A new one, that is. Sherbet's second body didn't look like the work of a legit vampire, but the first one definitely did. If a nut job saw the news talking about vampires and decided to kill someone for the thrill, doing it again so soon points to more of a spree killer or idiot than a methodical serial killer.

Still, a killer is a killer.

"Okay. I'll call him right away."

"Wait… Ma, did you say Nepal? Like, the country?"

"Yes. Oh, I found Milo. He's fine, just a—" Beep. Beep. "Call waiting. I think Sherbet's trying to call me. I'll explain face to face later. Weird story."

She laughs. "They always are. Glad he's okay. Stay safe!"

"You too."

"I will. Got the pepper spray right here. See you later."

"Bye." I click over to the other call. "Hello?"

"Sam," says Sherbet. "Been trying to get a hold of you."

"Yeah, sorry. Was just on the line with my

daughter. She called to say you called. I was out of coverage area... probably at least sixty miles from the nearest thing resembling a cellular tower."

"Oof. We got another one."

"Another vampire attack?" I ask.

"Superficially looks that way, but I have my doubts now. It looks more like the second victim. No scratching, just the neck wounds. Wanna take a look?"

"Yeah. I'll be there in a moment. Where exactly is it?"

"Behind the Wendy's on Orangethorpe in Buena Park."

I nod, even though he can't see me. "Yeah, I know the place. Massive parking lot, small Wendy's."

He clears his throat. "Yep. That's the one. I'd say you should hurry before the ME collects the remains, but I suspect you'll literally be here in a moment."

"Good instincts."

We share a laugh and hang up.

Ugh, great, another dead person.

I stuff my phone back in my purse and catch sight of the Hello Kitty keychain I found near the other crime scene. Not to be too judgmental, but a keychain like that does generally suggest the owner is a girl. Since I know Milo's not running around biting people in a blind panic, my mental image of the theoretical kid vampire becomes that of a young woman. Or at least a small one… a girl Tammy's size, maybe. For all I know, it could be a little old lady, too. Then again, the perfume scent on the keychain doesn't conjure images of a sweet old grandma. It's somewhere between Walmart perfume little kids might play with and the liquid sleaze the girls at Danny's former adult club might bathe in.

Two neat punctures. Hmm. Maybe she's working on her manners now and not shredding the bodies? Nah. Doesn't feel right. A vampire shouldn't have to feed this often unless they're getting their butt kicked severely. Self-healing requires energy. Energy equals blood.

Hmm. Do I go back to Nepal and get into a fight with yetis or go chasing a vampire?

Decisions… decisions.

I fish out the keychain and examine the hotel keycard. No writing on it except for that Aladdin lamp thing. This thing will lead me to either a killer or a witness who saw the killer. All I need to do is find out where it came from. I take a photo of the card and text it to Tammy, with a note asking her if she can do some internet sleuthing and maybe discover its origin.

And, well… since I have no idea where to start looking for a potentially dangerous rogue newbie vampire and I know exactly where to go for the yeti problem, I decide to deal with the hairy situation first.

Right after I take a look at Sherbet's body.

Ack. That sounded so wrong. Not Sherbet's actual body, the dead body he found.

Ugh, Sam. Get a grip.

I need more coffee.

Chapter Eighteen
Rabbit's Foot

There aren't too many more inglorious endings to a human life than to be found dumped in the parking lot behind a Wendy's.

No dig on Wendy's, just a fast-food joint in general... or a commercial area like this, downtown. How many people walked by the dead man, ignoring him because they assumed him a sleeping vagrant?

I teleport to a tiny clump of trees about 200 feet south of the restaurant. It stands at the southwest corner of an adjacent (much smaller) parking lot for a two-story commercial building with one of those red tile roofs people around here seem to like. The tree clump offers a bit of concealment for my sudden appearance out of nowhere. Unless yeti attacks and frost nymph sightings start to become a commonplace occurrence in California, I should really do as much as I can to keep my supernatural tricks hidden.

Even from this distance, it's obvious something is going on at the Wendy's. A bunch of police cars and officers congregate by the south side of the building where a little walled enclosure contains the restaurant's garbage dumpsters. Oh, poor guy. Even worse than being dumped next to a fast food joint... being dumped in its trash? Could be the killer intended it as concealment rather than insult. There isn't much else in the immediate area capable of concealing a body for long. The row of tiny knee-high shrubs around the drive-through lane won't do it.

Clock is ticking, so I hurry over to the police area. My 'consultant' badge gets me past the perimeter officers. That, plus Sherbet waving me over. The closer I get, the more intense my emotions become. This area is saturated in a feeling of angry urgency. My mood is shifting in response to outside forces. Detective Sherbet starts to talk to me, but I hold a hand up to stall him and keep approaching the dumpster enclosure... because it feels like it wants me to.

Not sure what the 'it' refers to. Not the dumpsters. The feeling, perhaps?

A dead man in a security guard uniform lays on the pavement in front of the dumpster. Three fat trash bags are scattered haphazardly nearby. The brown swinging gates attached to the white cinderblock walls hang open. My guess is a Wendy's employee found the body while attempting to take out the trash, screamed, threw the bags over their shoulder, and ran away.

It also feels like someone I can't see is staring at me.

This man's ghost is here. Gotta be. Except, I can no longer see the wavy, flowing energy that ghosts use to materialize.

I smell burnt fabric. Ozone. In the back of my mind, a man screams. It sounds far away.

Sherbet walks up beside me, waiting.

The dead man appears to be in his mid to late thirties. His uniform fits well enough to seem like it belongs to him, unlike the second body whose clothing didn't fit well. This man isn't a vagrant someone tried to pass off as someone else. I touch two fingertips to the back of his hand. The urgency comes from him. Late for work. Night shift, probably at that commercial building I just walked past... or something around here. His car is probably still close by.

"He died not far away," I say without really knowing why. "The killer used a stun gun on him."

"How do you know that?" whispers Sherbet.

"I can smell the burned fabric. Once you roll him over, you'll probably see the marks on the back of his shirt."

Sherbet crouches next to me and points at two puncture marks on the neck. "Looks like the second victim again. Fake?"

A nearby cop who overhears him rolls his eyes, as if a 'vampire bite' would be anything other than fake.

I lean closer to check on the marks. They're too small, neat, and perfect to have been made by fangs. Also, no indentations from other teeth between them. A sensation like an arm going around my neck from behind accompanies a burning feeling in my lower back. It's potent enough to make me brace a hand against the spot and draw a sharp breath.

"You all right, Sam?" asks Sherbet.

"Yeah." I wince. "Just picking up on some latent stuff. This was recent. The deceased is also quite angry. They wanted to fight back, but couldn't. He's furious."

"Sure he wasn't just in a bad mood havin' to go to work in the middle of the night?" asks the nearby officer.

I pull my hair off my face. "Possible. Not getting that much detail."

The guy smirks, unamused at my serious response to his attempt to poke fun at me.

Sherbet points my attention to blood spatter on the walls of the dumpster enclosure. The pattern is suggestive of arterial spurting, though not enough to be fatal. "We got a little bit of a break this time. Security cameras on the Wendy's captured the attack. Unfortunately, the killer's face isn't too visible. The deceased is walking across the parking lot. Another man comes up behind him, there's a brief struggle, then he's dragged out of sight—presumably to this enclosure."

"Ballsy. What time?"

"About midnight," says Sherbet. "The Wendy's was still open. Think they shut down at one in the morning. Guy did it while a few cars sat in the lane over here." He points to the nearby drive-thru.

"Damn." I shake my head in disbelief. "Crazy no one noticed, but I guess they would have had to turn around in their cars and look back." The drive-thru entry point is right in front of us. Cars would be going to the right. "Still brazen."

"More news." Sherbet glances over at the medical examiner's van arriving. "First victim died to exsanguination."

"The teacher," I say.

"Yep. Second man was strangled. Blood removal occurred after death."

"Sounds like two different killers. Only one of which is, uh… special."

Sherbet makes a face like he's about to quote *Lethal Weapon* and say he's getting too old for this shit, but he only sighs. "That's what I'm thinking, too. I managed to ID the second man. Greg Williams. Prints in the system, luckily. He's been transient for the past ten or so years. No fixed address. Near impossible to track down the last anyone saw him. This one had ID on him. Christopher Casey. He worked just across the way at night."

I lean over Mr. Casey to examine his face and neck for signs of strangulation. Sure enough, I spot telltale petechiae as well as finger-shaped bruises on the neck. "This man was strangled as well."

Sherbet pulls out a small flashlight, crouches next to me again, and spots the light on the victim's face.

"Petechiae." I point. "Bruises, too."

"Wow. Good eyes. Those are faint."

I feign innocence until he smiles at his unintentional joke about my vision being sharp. Yes, my eyes are very, very good. I point. "Check out the fang marks. Lower one is larger."

"Deformed vampire?" asks Sherbet in a nonserious tone.

"More likely, whoever made those holes used an awl or something similar and rushed the job," I say.

"That's consistent with victim number two," says Sherbet. "ME thinks the puncture wounds were left by a metal implement. We got a vampire wanna-be psycho. Bite marks on the first victim weren't the same. ME listed them as undetermined origin, likely animal."

I stand and back away as the medical examiner team arrives to take custody of the body. "Sounds about right."

Sherbet checks with his associates to make sure

they're all done photographing the dead security guard and everything around him, then gives the medical examiner's people the go-ahead to remove the remains from the scene. While they do that, he steps back to stand beside me and watch. "Thinking the first one's genuine and inspired a copycat."

"Yeah," I whisper. "If this keeps up, hunters might start sniffing around."

"That a bad thing?" asks Sherbet, almost chuckling.

"Not necessarily. At least, not for me. It might make life a bit awkward for some people I know."

He whistles. "Maybe they'll solve our problem for us."

"Maybe. Heh. They're almost better at finding vampires than I am."

"Supernatural instinct or something?" Sherbet raises an eyebrow at me.

"Yeah, something like that. Whatever it is, they're born with it... and damn good at their job. Scary good." I fish the keyring and card out of my purse. "Gonna have to get lucky and figure out where this came from."

"Luck, huh? Where's your rabbit's foot?" He smiles.

"I left that in Hillcrest Park one night fourteen some odd years ago."

"When you were attacked?"

"Yep." Honestly, I can't say if my 'luck' after that night has been good or bad. It's subject to perspective. I hold up the key card. "Have you seen this symbol before?"

"Just on that Disney movie." He gets a wistful smile. "Zayn still loves those movies. Is that like a side effect?"

I almost laugh. "No. Being gay doesn't make a person any more or less likely to enjoy cartoon movies... though it might make them less prone to lying about liking them."

He makes this 'oh yeah' face. "That, uhh, toxic masculinity stuff, right?"

"You've been reading, I see."

"Hey now, don't accuse me of being an intellectual or something." He winks. "So, you're saying I have actual work to do now. One vamp and one normal psychopath."

"Looks that way." I drop the keychain back in my purse. "Any connection between the second two victims?"

"Hey, we just got started on this one, but doesn't look like it. Only thing that comes to mind is they both would've been outside, alone, at night."

I exhale a long, slow breath. "Yeah. Opportunist killer. Also striking pretty close together. Either an idiot or arrogant and thinks he can get away with it."

Sherbet shakes his head. "The hardest ones to solve are when the victims are completely random strangers with no connection to the killer."

"Yeah."

"My fear here..." Sherbet folds his arms. "Is we're looking at another 'Night Stalker' type situation. If this guy keeps killing at random, the news is going to get a hold of it and we're looking at panic again. People afraid to go outside at night, and so on."

I nudge him. "You're more worried about this going on and on and having to retire before you find the son of a bitch."

"That, too." He grumbles. "I'd much prefer not having an unsolved case hanging on me whenever I get around to retiring, but I ain't near close to that yet."

Poor guy. He's not ready to give up the hunt. I really hope he decides to rest before something happens that forces him to. At his age, it's fairly easy to suffer a retirement-causing injury.

Sherbet's not a big fan of the sympathetic look I'm giving him—or so says his expression. "Look here, missy. I'm not old."

"I didn't say that."

"You thought it."

"I thought you deserve to have a nice chunk of time to enjoy life *before* you get old." I pause to let the medical examiner people go by with the dead man on a stretcher. "This case won't plague you for twenty years. You have something the Night Stalker detectives didn't."

"Oh? What's that?" He sets his fists on his hips, staring at me expectantly. "You?"

"Well, that, too… but I was thinking more along the lines of Allison, too. Maybe she can see something."

"Your witch friend?" He chuckles, shaking his head. "At this point, I'll take all the help I can get."

Chapter Nineteen
An Abominable Situation

Between my psychic intuition and an inconveniently aimed security camera, we're at least certain the vampire copycat killer is a man.

Sure, it's possible for women to reach over six feet in height, but not exactly common. It's less common for a female killer to ambush attack total strangers in a parking lot. Historically, women who kill tend to rely on guile rather than brute force.

Less scientifically, the energy on the victim felt male.

I find myself momentarily thinking about whether or not Christopher Casey—the dead guy behind the Wendy's—had a guardian angel and if so, what sort of excuse did they come up with for abandoning their post? This, of course, brings me back to the philosophical debate I had with Max some months ago regarding angels. Could be, they exist to escort people to their predetermined fate rather than protect them from *all* harm. But if that's true, and everything that happens to us is predetermined, I really need to have some words with whoever is writing the script, so to speak.

Well, no sense driving myself crazy asking questions that are impossible to answer.

Might as well take advantage of the Wendy's being right here. Once my presence is no longer needed at the crime scene, I go into the restaurant and grab something to eat. No, I'm not interested in a burger and fries.

Despite a murder investigation going on by the drive-in lane, the place is still rather full. Only one guy yawns when I siphon energy off the crowd in line to order. As a matter of principle, I omit the workers from the process. They need every ounce of energy they have to put up with this job, the management, and the customers. The effect of my feeding on people often results in a few seconds of mental blankness. Everyone is too zoned out to realize they all did so at the same time.

It's also the perfect opportunity for me to slip unnoticed into the hallway leading to the bathrooms. A lavatory in a fast-food restaurant is hardly the most lavish place, but it is enclosed and private: perfect as a launchpad for teleportation. Hopefully, this place doesn't have an overly attentive security manager who will notice me on video walking into the bathroom and never leaving. Maybe I'll end up YouTube famous without anyone knowing who the 'mysterious Wendy's woman' is by name.

As soon as I close the door, I summon the single flame, focusing on the distant village in Nepal.

My view through the little opening in the fire shows the village quiet, most of the people having gone inside again. The frost nymph appears to be standing guard near the edge of the village facing the forested area. She looks worried, a trace annoyed, and a little bit frightened as well.

When I leap through the expanding ring of fire in my mind and appear next to her, she jumps back, startled.

"Sorry, it took me longer than I thought it would. Something came up." I squeeze my hands into fists and shiver at the sudden shift from California weather to twenty below or whatever the heck it is up here.

Worry leaves her expression, but she still looks mildly annoyed.

"Hey." I hold my arms out to either side. "I told you I'd be back. Here I am. Couldn't leave the boy stranded away from his family when he's got nothing to do with this."

"Very well. You did return." She folds her arms. The delicate patterns of frost along her skin catch the sunlight, gleaming as she moves.

I rub my hands up and down my sides and arms.

Pretty sure this area didn't get colder, but standing next to this being who's wearing a damn-near-translucent minidress is making the temperature seem much worse. "Maybe I should've stopped somewhere and got a coat."

She touches my shoulder. A spray of snowy white stuff swirls around me... and it no longer feels freezing here. "No need."

"Thank you." I gaze down at myself. Nothing looks different. "Neat. So, umm, what are we dealing with? You said it's one man?"

"Yes." She turns to face the woods, staring into them. For a moment, the only sound other than the distant moan of the wind over the peaks is the delicate icy clinking of her hair. "An outsider has come, searching for an ancient power nexus. He has not found it yet. If he does, many innocent people will pay the price."

I scan the woods. Nothing appears unusual. It's quite beautiful to be honest... even if the presence of a forest here seems a little strange. Caught by the sudden sense of weirdness, I pull my phone out and check the GPS app. The map isn't showing any green stuff here. It just looks like open white mountain terrain.

"Is that forest natural? Or..." I look around. "Are we somewhere else?"

The nymph smiles. "All that exists is natural. I do not understand what you mean by unnatural."

I show her the phone screen as if a nymph

would have any idea what she's looking at. "This map doesn't show any trees around here. Why is there a forest?"

"Do you trust your map or your eyes?"

"There's a question." I glance at the screen, then the woods. "Usually, I'd say my eyes."

"You doubt."

"I do."

Her smile spreads into a grin. "There are places where the veil between realms is thin. People can drift back and forth."

"Oh, hang on. This is starting to sound a lot like that, uhh…" I scratch my head. "Hoia-Baciu forest… in Romania? Something about a little girl disappearing without a trace only to reappear five years later and *still* be only five years old?"

"It may be similar. If the story you speak of is true, the child momentarily left what you call the 'normal world.' She may have traversed to the fey realm, where time is disconnected from here. She experienced only a few minutes to a few hours before wandering back out of the forest."

"Right…" I gaze back at the village. "Is this village real, then? Wait, obviously, it is. I mean… are we in the normal world or in some other one?"

"We are at a place where two realities coexist." The nymph points south. "Far in that direction there live many people who regard this village as a folklore tale and not real. There are protections—from my people—that lead travelers astray, so they never find this place. It is here and real, but they simply walk around it."

I nod. "You're protecting this nexus thing. Ley lines?"

Her expression brightens. "You are familiar?"

"Sorta." I tilt my hand in a so-so gesture. "I have some, uhh, *past* experience with them. Really past."

She tilts her head in confusion. "You are not so old."

"I'm talking time travel. I try not to think about it too much, so my brain doesn't melt. Had to activate a ley line to fling myself forward back to my actual time."

"Oh." She grimaces. "It is dangerous to meddle with the power flowing through the Earth's veins if you are inexperienced in doing so."

Heh. I offer a weak smile. "Guess I got lucky then. So, this guy… he's looking for a ley line nexus. What's your plan then? Chase him off? Go in there and kick his ass?"

"I do not think kicking him in the rear end would help." She blinks at me.

It takes all my willpower not to burst out laughing at her baffled expression. "Sorry. I don't mean literally hoof him in the backside. It's a phrase. Do you plan to kill him?"

"Oh." She furrows her eyebrows at me as if to ask what the hell 'kicking an ass' has to do with murder, then seems to dismiss the thought with a faint eye roll. Yes, humans are weird. "We must do something. My kind cannot continue holding them back. He is... shockingly powerful for a mortal."

"Them? The yetis?"

"No, the yetis are conjurations. Tools, only." She again points at the woods. "This man, who other humans know as Kratos Dimitris, is the head of an order of diabolists. They are mortals who cavort with demons."

I stifle a groan. "Yeah, I'm familiar with the term diabolist. Ran into them before... I think. Cult summoning a bunch of tentacle-faced monstrosities. Bad people. Worse hosts. They always serve those stale, flavorless cookies and weak coffee."

She gives me side eye as though she can't tell if I'm kidding or not. The expression is almost perfect Tammy. It's the same look she gets on her face whenever her inability to interpret body language/ social cues leaves her stuck wondering what someone means. Even though this nymph is probably hundreds of years old, she looks about the same age as my daughter, maybe even a little bit younger.

It's good to be an elf, I guess. Or... nymph.

Hmm. Maybe the whole humanity hating vampires thing is a conspiracy from a consortium of powerful cosmetics manufacturers and plastic surgeons. If people don't get old, they'd lose a lot of money.

Absurdity aside, I have work to do here.

"So, diabolists are here?" I raise an eyebrow.

"Strange they are summoning fake yetis instead of demons, but hey… I'll take it."

The nymph emits a soft bell-like sigh, her breath like a distant set of crystalline wind chimes. "This group had little power until not so long ago when they experienced a massive resurgence of power. My kind sensed a great disturbance in the magical fabric of the world, as if an ocean had been drained and abruptly refilled."

"Oops," I deadpan. "My bad."

She glances at me. "Why do you say this? Does it not mean you made a mistake? How could you have possibly caused a surge of magic into the world?"

"It's a long, complicated story… probably enough to fill a whole book or two." I catch a glimpse of something white moving in the trees, likely a yeti. "Can't explain now… here they come."

The nymph flicks her gaze into the woods, spots the creature, and starts running toward it. She holds her arms out, fingers spread. Blue light gathers beneath her palms. Snow peels up from the ground, whirling into the shapes of two small, curved swords.

Neat trick.

And dammit. I didn't grab a weapon. My knuckles ache merely from thinking about punching one of those damn yeti again. I'd complain about this psychic vampire form not including claws, but they wouldn't help here, anyway. At least, not much. I could tell by punching these things they have thick hides, plus dense fur. Vampire claws might be supernaturally sharp, but they're still only like an inch long. Maybe I'm underestimating them since I never really super-adored being an undead monster.

Pointless, since it's not an option. Besides, I'd much rather *not* be undead. It's way easier for me to carry a knife or something and not rely on claws than for an undead vampire to negotiate peace with the sun.

For now, I follow the nymph, since she's brandishing two ice swords.

The yeti in question appears to be alone... and it doesn't last long. When she isn't having to defend herself against six of them at once, she's free to dance around the monster. I almost feel bad for it, as it's so profoundly slow it has no chance. She slices the heck out of it in seconds, finishing with a killing stab straight up into the underside of its jaw. Before she can even pull her weapon out of the corpse, the faux-yeti has disintegrated into a hanging smoke cloud.

I'm sure if one of the yetis managed to hit her, she'd be in serious trouble. She looks kind of brittle and delicate. Let's hope she's fast enough to keep out of their reach.

"This way," she whispers, before hurrying off.

Chapter Twenty
Blade

Keeping up with her is a serious chore.

It started off damn near impossible thanks to thigh-deep snow. Well, I'm sure it's way deeper than that, but it's been here so long it's become dense enough that I *only* sink in thigh deep. The top three-ish feet is airy enough to swallow most of my legs. There is a reason humanity invented snow-shoes. The nymph, unsurprisingly, glides effort-lessly across the snowy surface without even mak-ing tracks.

As soon as I give up on walking and sprout wings, it's much easier to follow her. Kinda rare for me to feel slow. I'm used to being significantly faster than ordinary humans. While the difference between her and me isn't as big as between me and humans, it's definitely frustrating to feel like I'm that straggler kid at the back of the line who has to constantly yell 'wait for me' at the rest of the campers.

I don't yell 'wait for me.' Just saying.

Once we reach the forest, the snow isn't as much of an issue. The trees keep enough of the white stuff off the ground to where I no longer need to rely on my wings keeping me from sinking into the drifts.

We race among the pines for only a few minutes before the nymph slows from 'Paxton in the mall' speed to a more cautious, stealthy approach. Now, it's easy to keep up with her. The two of us sneak along for a short while more. Soon, the murmurs of distant voices reach my awareness along with lots of grunting and... some other noise. It's not a real word but the best thing I can think of to describe it is 'snorfling.' Whatever it is, the sound is coming from yetis. Can't tell if they are snoring, picking their noses, having a moment of ecstasy over the perfect snowball, or what.

The nymph takes cover in a copse of trees, crouching amid the icy undergrowth. Looking at her still makes me shiver—she's basically running around barefoot in a dress as insubstantial as a silk chemise. Makes sense if she's a *frost* nymph, though. What's that line from the movie Paxton adores? 'The cold never bothered me, anyway'?

Something like that.

I crouch beside her and follow her stare to a surprisingly large encampment. Several tents as well as a few wooden shacks surround a central clearing containing a fairly crude statue made of bundled branches. Hard to say if the antler-like projections sticking out from either side of its head are supposed to be a hat or if the entity depicted has horns. What it lacks in detail it makes up for in size, being about twelve feet tall.

A hollow in the statue's chest contains a glowing violet orb seemingly made of frosted glass. I estimate it to be about the size of a basketball. It's also throwing off energy, enough for me to feel. The primitivism of the effigy makes it impossible for me to recognize as any specific god, demon, or whatever, but it's undoubtedly intended as an object of tribute to whatever demonic master this Kratos guy serves.

Hmm. Sounds Greek. Maybe I should ask Max what he knows about diabolist cults from Greece? This might be more significant than a simple random group of power-crazed idiots. Then again, one could arguably refer to Elizabeth and her followers as a 'random group of power-crazed idiots.'

We must have arrived during a lull or something, as there are no people in sight. If anyone's here, they're inside the tents or shacks. However, about twenty yetis stand around the encampment. They occasionally meander back and forth, but for the most part, stand in place. I can't help but think of Anthony's video games… specifically, how the 'monsters' tend to just stand there doing nothing until a player attacks them. Heh. I guess video game AI and magical summoning AI are pretty similar. These aren't 'real' yetis after all.

"Hey," I whisper. "Do you have a name? Or should I just refer to you as 'the frost nymph'?"

A hint of amusement shines through her overall sense of worry. "I am Nyali."

"Hi. I'm Sam."

"I know." Nyali shifts her attention back to the camp.

I smirk at her wiseass comment, even if she isn't intending to be a wiseass. When she grins back, it's obvious she did intend to be a wiseass. Poor girl seems to be seriously nervous and trying to hide it. And yeah, she's gotta be centuries old. Just looks like a teenager to me. Probably shouldn't think of her as a 'girl.'

"I don't see any people. What do you think we should do?" I ask.

Nyali points at the orb glowing from within the statue's chest cavity. "It may be good fortune none of the diabolists are expecting visitors. The large crystal is the source of the man's unusually strong power. Humans are not so magically gifted—at least not anymore."

"Not anymore?" I raise an eyebrow.

She looks at me, the pale blue light in her eyes flickering. "A thousand years ago, humans possessed much more magic. They have abandoned it for machines as they have abandoned nature for great cities built of dead rock."

"Isn't all rock dead?"

"No… I…" She scowls in frustration. "Struggle with your words. It is not rock, but rock the humans make from paste."

"Concrete?"

She shrugs as if to say 'maybe,' then nods. "I think so. When the magical surge happened recently, some humans who did not abandon the old ways reawakened. Not all are dangerous, but this one is."

"Okay. So, we yoink the orb?"

"I do not know what you mean by yoink." She blinks.

"Grab it and run?"

"Oh." She covers her mouth to suppress a laugh. "No. We must destroy it. This orb is demonic. Without it, Kratos will be powerless to control the yeti and no threat to the village."

And he won't bring magic and supernatural stuff into the forefront of societal consciousness, and thus set off a nuclear war. Got it. So, yeah. Good idea to stop this guy. "Please tell me you know how to destroy it?"

Nyali beams. "I do. But first, there is magic in you, but you struggle to reach it."

Before I can ask her to go into greater detail, she reaches out and places her hand on my forehead, as if she's checking me for a fever. Her voice manifests in my head whispering words in a language incomprehensible to me. Cold tingles down the nerves in my arms, followed by a full-body chill... like I'd just gone skinny dipping in a Siberian lake in the middle of February. It's *so* shockingly cold and sudden I can't even gasp.

Thankfully, the sensation lasts only a fraction of a second.

"Wha...?" I shiver. "What was that?"

Nyali takes my hand and holds it out toward the snow. "I have given you magic. Tell the water and the snow to help you."

I shouldn't know this, but for some reason, I know she's telling me to imagine gathering snow into a sword. The nymph must have somehow infused knowledge directly into my head. Nothing feels as bizarre as doing something that comes as easily as instinct, yet feels brand new.

Here goes...

Almost as soon as I want it to happen, snow vaporizes up from the ground to gather in the approximate outline of an English longsword. Seconds later, it condenses into a solid—and very real—ice sword. It looks like something you'd see at Comic-Con or straight out of one of Anthony's video games. The blade is ocean blue at the core, lightening to cyan at the edges. Fairly sure it's glowing. The light coming from the blade is a little too strong to simply be it catching ambient daylight, but it's not *so* bright as to be definitely an inexplicable glow.

I hold the weapon vertically in front of my face and stare through the translucent blade at the trees we're hiding behind. It's a bit on the lighter side, weight wise. Doesn't feel like a genuine weapon as much as a costume prop made of dense plastic. Unlike a prop, though, the edge *looks* sharp. Nyali's whispery presence in the back of my mind seems to be responsible for me knowing how this thing works. All the information hits me at once, as if I'd known it for most of my life.

The weapon is temporary. It will last as long as I need it to, then melt back into water. I can make it take any shape I want from dagger to scimitar, curved or straight, short or long. No doubt its present form came from my time with Sebastian. Okay, my inner warrior is having a moment. It's cool to have a sword in my hand again.

Ugh. Cool. Sorry. I didn't mean that pun.

"With this, you can destroy the orb," says Nyali. "Ordinary weapons will not harm it."

I eye the blade, then the orb, then her. "It's just sitting there out in the open. You needed my help with this? Not that I mind, really. I'm already here. Just… confused."

She nods, her expression shifting apologetic. "The shrine is warded against my kind. Foul enchantments will kill me if I get too close. There are also traps."

"Okay. Yeah, seems kinda dumb for this dude to leave the source of his power sitting outside in the open where anyone could grab it." I heft my new ice sword, getting used to the feel of its weight. It's going to swing faster than a metal blade. Not too much of a worry at the moment unless the diabolists have weapons too. Good chance a big crystal ball isn't going to try to parry me. "Just to make sure I understand, all I need to do is get in there and give the magic ball a good clobbering with this sword?"

She nods. "Don't worry if your weapon breaks. You can just make a new one."

"Good to know."

"I will cause a distraction and lure the yeti away." Nyali stands, pointing to the east.

"Not sure how I feel about storming in there and killing some guy, even if he is a murderer." I stand as well. "But… if it has to be done or he's going to kill more innocent people."

Nyali shakes her head, causing her long icicle hair to clatter. "We do not need to slay him, merely take away his power."

"Okay." I smile. "That, I can do."

Chapter Twenty-one
A Matter of Delicate Violence

From where I stand, I figure it would be fairly easy to just teleport the 150 feet or so to the statue and whack the orb. None of the yetis are close enough to get in the way.

However, Nyali mentioned wards and traps. While I don't totally understand magic, witchcraft, or things of that nature much, it does sound like a bad idea to mix teleportation with an enchanted area. The last thing I need is to end up blowing myself into smithereens, or end up bouncing off and careening into some other crazy destination it will take me forever to find my way out of… like another dimension or the innermost depths of an IKEA.

Traps also get me thinking of things like spring

loaded jaws or land mines—something to step on. Can't step on a landmine when flying, right?

Right. I leap onto my wings and fly over the five-or-six yetis between me and the stick statue.

The magical creatures don't notice me sail over their heads. Stupid yetis. I aim the sword point-first in front of me as I close in on the orb, ready to drive the ice blade into it... like stabbing the eyeball of a cyclops. Of which I was all too familiar.

As the gap between me and orb rapidly diminishes and I'm starting to think this most basic of plans just might work, a tremendous *boom* accompanies me smashing face-first into an invisible barrier sphere surrounding the statue. My vision lingers on a brief glimpse of something akin to a force field bursting right before the impact energy flings me into reverse. I land on my back and promptly flip into a tumble... reminiscent of a huge raven attempting to land like an airplane.

Problem is, ravens don't have wheels.

Second problem is, birds striking the ground at full speed tend to wipe out hard.

Thankfully, a nice, helpful yeti is there to slow my roll. I slam into his legs hard enough to bowl him over. He falls forward, crashing down on top of me. Luck is with me, though. He's too startled at the impact to try and grab me. Snow to the face mutes his startled roar. I can't see much but thick white fur pushing down on my face. Hey, at least he's soft.

People, mostly men, start shouting in alarm.

Dammit. So much for the element of surprise, right?

While I am probably strong enough to shove a yeti out of my way, being flat on my back with one on top of me is a severe leverage disadvantage. After two seconds, I understand I'm going nowhere via brute force until this yeti decides to get up. Alas, I neither have the time to wait nor the inclination to. A quick teleport—straight up ten feet—is enough to get me clear. I appear in midair and drop to land atop the same yeti, making him grunt.

"Hey. I'm not *that* heavy," I grumble.

Nyali stares at me from the edge of the camp on my right. Her expression is mostly worry, but there's a note of 'what the heck are you doing?' in there as well. Okay, so the barbarian charge at the orb didn't work. So much for traps being ground based. Guess flying isn't going to help me either. Hopefully, the force-field that kicked me away is expended and won't happen again. It did appear to have popped like a massive bubble.

Bigger problem: six people in massively thick parkas have emerged from various tents and rickety shacks. None of them are rushing toward me, though. Worse is, they're waving their arms around and chanting. Pretty sure they're using magic.

I've seen Allison throw lightning bolts, and I've seen what those lightning bolts did to whatever she nailed. Ugh. This isn't going to end well.

The yeti I'm standing on emits another *oof* when I step over him to the ground and rush for the statue.

Another yeti lunges at me from the left. I duck its enormous hands and reflexively maneuver into an attack, thrusting my ice longsword into its ribcage. The creature bursts into smoke. In the same instant, a barrage of icicles whistle past my face.

I turn to glare at whoever chucked them at me… but there's no one there. In fact, I'm pretty sure they appeared out of thin air from the vicinity of the statue. Crap. Another ward spell or something. The statue itself is trying to kill me. Whatever magic Kratos infused it with seems to know I'm a threat.

Most of the yetis swarm east to chase Nyali since they spotted her first thanks to my aerial jump. The critters do seem to be rather dumb, fixating on the first thing they saw. Glowing blue comets of ice come flying at me from the human wizards, though one of them decides on a more mundane means and pulls out a gun.

Three yetis who happen to be closer to me are still an issue. Ugh. Fur on one side, ice on the other, and some jackass with a handgun. He's a bit too far away to use it immediately, so he comes running at me, gun aimed, shouting in… either Russian or Greek. I can't tell if he's trying to order me to get away from the statue or he'll shoot… or he's saying he's going to rip out my heart and feed it to his de-monic pet.

Probably doesn't matter. Not like I'm going to

just give up and go home and let these people continue to kill innocent villagers and set off a chain of events that could end—or drastically reshape—society across the globe.

I disregard him for now and get into a swordfight with the yetis. They are so damn slow it's easy to weave around their clumsy punches and stab them to 'death.' I go from one to the next, ramming the blade as deep as I can before ripping it away from dissipating clouds of smoke. Sticking almost four feet of ice blade into their hearts is *way* easier than attempting to punch them. I'm almost ashamed of myself for feeling a sense of exhilaration at deadly combat. This ice blade is seriously sharp. Way sharper than I'd expect from ice, or even steel. It's also remarkably tough. You'd think stabbing what's essentially a massive icicle into a 900-pound snow-squatch would break it. Nope. It's holding up just fine.

I could really do without the constant pelting of ice daggers coming from the statue area and the occasional walloping of potato-sized ice chunks striking me in the back and legs. The yetis surrounding me do provide a good deal of cover from icy projectiles. Yeti by yeti, I kill my way closer to the statue.

The tenth time I kill a critter, I realize I'm having a bit of a math problem.

I charged at three yetis. In a chaotic whirlwind of dodging and stabbing, I killed... ten yetis?

Something's not adding up.

That's the moment I realize two of the humans —including the guy with the gun—have given up trying to hit me with ice comets and are conjuring more yetis. Much the same as when I made the sword, the snow blasts up into a giant, humanoid shape and condenses into a yeti. It appears to take them about six seconds per yeti to make new ones. According to Allison, using magic is about the same as performing work. Some spells are more draining than others. Unfortunately, these guys look like they could keep pumping out yetis all day long.

I don't have that kind of time.

"Excuse me, one moment," I say to the nearest yeti right before dodging the enormous blue hand he's trying to clamp around my head. "Be right back."

I teleport about thirty feet away to a point between and slightly behind the two dudes making yetis and sending them after me. The ward spells around the statue continue chucking ice daggers at where I used to be, pelting a group of now nine highly confused yetis. As the big creatures begin digging at the snow trying to figure out where I went, I stick the ice sword in the ground beside me, grab the two guys, and yank them around to face me.

Both blurt in whatever language they speak. I don't understand them, but, 'Gah! Holy shit!' is fairly universal. Kingsley would smash their heads together or rip them open. I'm far too nice for my own good sometimes. Rather than break them in half, I unload my psychic feeder at full blast. This process does not usually manifest in a visible way... but I hit these guys so hard it creates a phantasmal white ether streaming out from their faces into my mouth.

Six seconds is all it takes to knock them out.

They'll probably sleep for three days.

Tingles run all down my body, where it rapidly heals bruises, shallow stab wounds, and maybe a cracked rib or two. In the distance behind me, the grunts of yetis and angry shouts of people tell me Nyali is still causing a distraction. I should hurry up so she can get out of here.

I rush for the statue, ducking ice comets which appear out of thin air and rocket toward me. The yetis finally notice me and stop tearing up the ground. Dammit. They're going to get in my way. Grr.

Nothing for me to do but to go full William Wallace here.

Next thing I know, I'm up to my eyeballs in angry yeti. Five have become fifteen. They're freakin' everywhere. It doesn't matter how easy they are for me to kill, they're proving to be an endless barrier, keeping me away from the statue. Grr. Another diabolist or two have to be summoning them. They've caught on to Nyali's ruse and are moving to address the real threat... *me*.

They'd have to know she can't go anywhere

near the orb, so it would be foolish for a frost nymph to even try attacking their camp.

Cold mist blasts me in the face. Tiny ice crystals rain from the exploding yetis as I kill one after the next, trying to go faster and outpace the summoning. My world is a blinding haze of snow and ape-like grunting. It's like I'm at a college frat party in the Eighties—wait, that's a different kind of snow.

A brilliant blue-white flash goes off around me. Something slams into me from below. In an instant, I find myself more or less paralyzed, off my feet, and freezing. The yetis stop trying to pound me into mush and stare. It occurs to me they're no longer looking down at me. We're at eye level. The next thing I notice is a buttload of extreme pain.

I glance down at myself.

Mistake.

A bloom of massive icicles has erupted from the ground below me. I'm impaled on needles the size of small trees. They angle up from the ground, converging to meet somewhere around where my hips are, then expand outward as they go up. At least seven of them pass *through* my body. I can't lift myself up off them due to the angle. For the same reason, I'm not sinking down on them. The biggest one is only about four inches in diameter. Four inches doesn't sound like much until it's impaled through your gut. I think the one sticking me in the left leg broke the femur.

Shit. This is not good.

The ice blade drops out of my hand since my fingers have stopped talking to me.

Ice javelins spear through both my arms, both my legs, and my torso. Holy shit, this hurts. I haven't been this uncomfortable since my parents forced me to participate in the talent show at my grade school.

In fact, the pain is so intense I'm on the verge of passing out. Wow. I didn't think my body was capable of passing out anymore. Guess I really am closer to being alive now.

For some reason I can't even begin to understand, the yetis merely stare at me... killer robots turned to an idle setting. Soft crunching comes from my left. I can't move my body, arms, or legs much at all. I could turn my head but it hurts too much.

A man meanders around to stand in front of me, making faces as if admiring his latest ice sculpture. He's wearing a heavy parka with a fur-lined hood. His face is, however, uncovered. Guy looks late forties. Big eyebrows. Weird, black paint on his face... or were those tattoos? Hard to tell from my position. And, oh yeah, his eyes are also glowing bright red.

"Ahh, Samantha," he says in perfect English. "I have been waiting for you."

"Waiting for me?" I blink.

"Indeed." The man I assume to be Kratos nods once. "My patron demanded your life as payment for his boon to me."

"Your... demon?"

"But of course." He holds his hands out to the sides in a 'behold my kingdom' sort of gesture. "Do you honestly believe some inconsequential child just happened to inherit a new house with a magical mirror in the attic, by chance? The demons know you, Samantha Moon. To catch a fish only required the correct sort of worm on the hook. In your case, a defenseless child."

I growl, struggling to move. Freezing ice spears impaling my body are much less comfortable when agitated, but I keep straining to break at least one of them. Intense pain threatens to blank out my vision to a haze of white.

A bizarre roaring noise—like a bonfire—draws my attention to the side. Turning my head to look hurts... trivial compared to everything else. Nyali is curled up in a ball, trapped in a flaming sphere. The look she gives me is entirely apologetic. She's not at all worried about herself... she's sorry she got me hurt. Or worse.

"The two of you shall be the first," says Kratos. "Your souls will power the great reawakening."

"Sorry, pal." I roll my head back to stare at him. "My soul's kinda spoken for already."

He smiles, then pulls his sleeves apart to reveal a wicked single-edged dagger. "You do not understand, Samantha. Your soul is fully contained. It is much, *much* more powerful than an ordinary person."

Consciousness clinging by a thread, I barely

have the energy to scream at him as he raises the knife like he's about to plunge it into my heart. Dread saturates me. The blade, of course, is laced with silver.

My vision starts to fade. Unconsciousness approaching fast.

No…

I can't let myself die here. My kids need me. I'm not ready to go away.

"Farewell, Samantha," says Kratos—as he thrusts the knife downward at my heart.

Chapter Twenty-two
Could've Gone Better

With my last bit of conscious strength, I cling to the thought of my kids and summon the single flame. A very weak flame is all I can muster.

As a flash of fire washes over me, a faint nip of pain picks at my sternum.

Everything goes dark. The cold is gone. It's almost hot here. I'm… elsewhere. The fire recedes out in front of me as a ring. My dancing flame gate. It worked. Except... I have no idea where I sent myself to. Could be anywhere. I just had to go away. And judging by the burning pain in my chest where the blade nicked me... I got away just in time.

But where?

Kingsley takes shape from within the burning flame. I stare at the man reclining on his sofa, aglow in the castoff light from his giant TV screen. Somehow, someway, I made the leap to his home... until I remember how.

It had been Kingsley's idea. To always have his home bookmarked in the back of my mind in case of an emergency. No need to summon an image. Sometimes, there's not even time for that.

Like this time.

Except... I'm not all the way there. Not yet.

"Sam?" He leaps to his feet. "What the hell is going on?"

I hold out my bloodied hand. He reaches for it and pulls. I have only enough strength left to stare at him for half a second before the rug rushes up to greet my face.

***

Next thing I know, I'm awash in silk.

I smell soap... and Kingsley. Consciousness expands, allowing me to feel myself lying naked in bed. Spots of dull, throbbing ache tell me wherever the ice pierced my body. Can't call it pain, more annoying.

When I open my eyes, I find Kingsley seated in a wingback chair beside the bed, his face lit by the glow from a Kindle. A buildup of delivery food containers tells me he's been standing guard over me for a while. Damn. How long has it been? Is Nyali still alive? Are my kids freaking out?

As soon as he notices me looking around, Kingsley practically chucks the Kindle over his shoulder and leans forward, resting his big, warm hand on my forehead. Relief, love, and anger mix in his eyes along with a faint yellow glow. He's deeply furious, no doubt itching to ask me who did this to me so he can go eat them. Almost any other time, I'd totally try to talk him out of it... but Kratos has sold himself to demons to the point his damn eyes light up red. Good clue there he doesn't count as an 'innocent human' anymore.

"Sam..."

"Hey, big guy. Thanks for the assist."

He pulls me up into his arms, transferring me from bed to sitting across his lap in the large chair. I'm still wrapped from armpit to toes in red silk sheets.

"What happened, Sam?"

"Charged into a situation half-assed." I don't bother trying to move yet. It's nice to be held. Also, he's so damn warm.

"Can you give me a little more detail than that?" He bows his head, pressing his forehead to mine.

We share a moment, just basking in our love for each other.

I curl up into him, resting my head on his shoulder. "How long was I out?"

"A day."

"You ate all that in one day?"

"Yes. You were hungry, too." He does air

quotes around the word hungry. "Being in the same room with you was… tiring." He chuckles. "I kept ordering delivery food so you could have something more than me to feed on. There's twice as much as this in the fridge. Don't worry, I'll get them back home safe."

"Get *who* back home safe?" I ask, suddenly nervous.

"The dozen or so Uber Eats drivers I've got stacked up in the living room, unconscious."

I stare at him. "Twelve delivery drivers came here and never returned? The cops are probably on the way right now."

He cracks and ends up laughing. "I'm teasing you. No one passed out… though they did leave rather groggy."

"You told the kids something?"

"Yes. They know you got hurt and are recovering." Kingsley leans back in the chair, throwing off such a sense of relief I suspect he might have been worried I wouldn't wake up. "So, what *did* happen to you?"

I let out a long, groaning breath… then explain the whole situation with Milo, the mirror, Nepal, the nymph, and Kratos, the red-eyed-demoniac. Oh, speaking of which… I really should call the Boones and tell them it might not be a bad idea to get out of that house. Kratos said something to the effect the inheritance was suspicious. Maybe Kaitlyn only believes she had an eccentric father who lived in Cali-

fornia, and that house is a demonic construct. Or...
maybe the demons simply hurried things along and
caused her mother's early demise. Either way, the
place has been touched by demons. Sure, it's possible to cleanse, but the kids hate it there, anyway.
Demons are only going to feed on that sadness and
twist it. Once a demon gets a foothold inside a
house, it's a real task to get rid of it.

Dammit. I'm not supposed to be dealing with
demons anymore. Well, sure, I can say I retired.
That doesn't mean the demons I've pissed off along
the way are going to throw their hands up and leave
me alone. Maybe I won't make any *new* demonic
enemies, but the ones already out for my head aren't
going to stop. Ugh. Demon bullshit is going to
haunt me forever, like those phone calls trying to
tell me my car's extended warranty is about to ex-
pire. They'll just never stop.

"Can't sit still." I start to squirm at the sheets.
"Nyali might still be alive... but even if she isn't,
this guy is going to set off a chain of events that will
end in nuclear war."

Kingsley raises both eyebrows. "You do plan to
at least get dressed first, right? Sorry, the outfit you
arrived in was too shredded to save. Had to rip it off
you."

"You ripped my clothes off?" I glance at him.
"Shame I wasn't awake to enjoy that."

He stares.

"Seriously, though... I'm going to ask you to

help me deal with this guy."

"Damn right I am. Whoever this Kratos guy is, he's not going to enjoy meeting me."

I can count the number of times Kingsley has been angry enough to *feel* on one hand. As terrifying as it is to be in the presence of a werewolf so angry, that someone hurting me is the source of his anger fills me with warmth and reassurance. I let the sheet drop to the floor over to one of the guest room closets. I'm here often enough to keep a semi-full wardrobe, certainly enough to not have to charge back to Nepal in the buff. Besides, it's a good chance the magic Nyali used on me to stave off the cold has ended by now.

Might be wise to dress warm. I'm almost jealous of Kingsley. He's got an amazing fur coat whenever he wants it.

Built in, as they say.

Chapter Twenty-three
War Room

Nyali's faint voice whispers at the back of my mind, begging for help.

I can't tell if it's really her or if something demonic is playing games with me. While this Kratos guy certainly seemed hell bent (pun intended) on killing us both as some manner of sacrifice, it's certainly possible he's keeping the frost nymph alive to bait me into a return. The guy doesn't know me too well, which in this case is good. I'm not the sort of person to get metaphorically knocked down, say 'screw that' and walk away—especially when an entire village of innocent people is in danger.

There's that whole nuclear Armageddon thing, too.

Nyali didn't give me much of an idea how

rapidly the situation would escalate. While it's likely a safe bet to assume nuclear weapons won't start flying within the next three days or so, I'm not going to wait that long. Kratos doesn't need to use Nyali as a hostage to lure me back there. I'd go anyway. With any luck, he doesn't know this and maybe she's not dead yet.

One thing I don't want to do is walk into a trap. At the moment I start the process of teleporting with Kingsley back to Nepal, my warning bells go off. They keep ringing in my ears even after I stop, but it isn't a feeling like I'm in imminent danger. More that my current plan of action is unwise and deadly, not that something is about to land on my head.

As soon as I randomly ponder the idea of asking Allison to help out, the warning noise weakens.

"Huh… odd."

"What's that?" asks Kingsley, his eyebrows tilted in a 'why are you waiting' quizzical stare.

I explain the warning feeling. "Seemed like we'd have been going into a bad situation. I thought about Allie and the warning got weaker, but it is still here."

He scratches one finger at the side of his head. "Sounds obvious to me. You need reinforcements. I can't promise to be helpfully rational once I see the man who did that to you. Good chance I might do something recklessly violent."

Aww. I hug him. "There's definitely a place for reckless violence here. But we should likely balance it out with a bit of brainpower, too."

He starts to give me this 'you're not serious' look, no doubt assuming I'm talking about Tammy... then he remembers she's no longer the world's most powerful telepath. And hey, even if she *wasn't* the world's strongest telepath, she's my kid, so of course I'm going to call her that.

"Never thought to refer to Allie as brainpower," says Kingsley, chuckling. "I mean, the girl's not dumb, but she doesn't come off as a super genius either."

"Psychic?" I tap my head. "That kind of brain power."

Kingsley shifts his jaw to the left, his eyes saying, 'oh, right.' Yeah, he's angry. Barely containing it even. "We should bring Anthony along, too, then. Fire and ice?"

My turn to reactionarily protest before thinking. I only say 'but' about six times before my brain catches up to my heart. To me, my son is still a cute little innocent, defenseless child... at least, when he isn't in sight. It's rather difficult to think of him as a baby when he's right in front of me. Whatever he is now... immortal, proto-angel, something else entirely... my son is *definitely* far from helpless. In fact, he's kinda powerful. Though, with his decision to return home and 'stick around to protect his sisters,' I'm not sure how much, if any, of his angelic powers had to go in a box for later. Maybe none. Maybe he didn't really have much of it to begin with, other than the ability to know things he shouldn't have known.

And, you know, turn into a giant fireball with a sword of his own.

No sooner does Kingsley bring up the idea of my son going with us than my alarm sense stops.

"Okay. Let's gather the forces then." I let out a long, slow exhale.

"Allison is already at your place," says Kingsley.

I blink. "She is? Why?"

"Uhh… after you passed out, I called her to ask if she knew anything about glowing wounds."

That makes me fidget. "Did you say 'glowing wounds'?"

Kingsley pulls me into a tight embrace. "I did not enjoy seeing you like that. Yes, you had several holes entirely through your body. The inside glowed blue. She didn't know what that meant, but did say she had a feeling you'd need her at the house."

"Huh…" I squeeze the big guy back. "Didn't realize she's *that* kind of psychic."

"Which kind?"

"See the future kind."

He chuckles. "Probably not what she thought. She likely meant to be there for the kids."

"Oh crap." I stare up at him. "Did anyone tell Mary Lou? She's going to be losing her mind."

"I didn't." Kingsley grimaces. "Maybe your kids did."

Considering I told him the tip of a dagger capable of killing me broke the skin above my sternum before I collected enough mental focus to teleport myself out, he's staying *remarkably* composed. That said, the urgency to go rip things in half radiates off him like a giant pressure cooker in a *Tom & Jerry* cartoon about to explode and take out the whole house.

I nod once at him, continue squeezing, and teleport us to my living room.

Good thing I aimed for behind the couch. Paxton, Renae, and three of their friends are sprawled around watching a movie. None of the girls notice us appear out of thin air behind them.

Tammy, who's sitting at the dining room table behind us with Allison, blurts, "Mom!"

This makes all the thirteen-year-olds turn. They see Kingsley and me, and promptly emit shrieks of surprise. Renae is the most composed of the five. She merely twitches. Paxton is extremely vulnerable to jump scares. She screams the loudest, begins crying for a few seconds, then—upon realizing it's me and Kingsley—shifts to laughing. Her giggles last only a short while before she ends up staring at the big guy. She doesn't look frightened *of* him as much as worried about why he's so furious. Yeah, the kid's an empath. Kingsley is angry enough for *me* to feel it. He's got to be practically glowing red to her. Metaphorically, I mean. She doesn't see emotions like colored lights.

"Everything okay, Mom?" she asks.

"Just got to take care of a little problem."

"Just a little problem?"

I can't lie to my kid, not when she can feel our heated emotions. "Maybe a medium-sized problem. But nothing I can't handle."

She studies me some more, then smiles. "Be careful, please. I kinda like it here."

I chuckle. "I will. Swear."

"Say, where'd you guys come from, anyway?" blurts Averie—one of Pax's school friends.

"Came in through the back yard." Kingsley points a thumb over his shoulder. "Didn't mean to startle you girls."

The kids return their attention to the movie. Kingsley and I head over to the living room. Anthony pokes his head out of his room, spots me, then rushes down the hall to give me a hug, too. Tammy is too calm. This tells me Kingsley didn't give them any details about how badly I'd been messed up. My son's expression and the strength of his embrace suggest he somehow knows.

"Yeah, Ma." Anthony relaxes his grip around me. "I'm going with you."

"Wait, what?" asks Tammy. "Going where?"

Allison points at her while staring at me. "What she said."

"War room time," I mutter.

"Oh, hey, Sam." Allison snaps her fingers. "I got some info on that serial killer Sherbet's looking for."

"Good timing, but that will need to wait. Grab a winter coat. We're going to fight yetis."

She raises both eyebrows. "You got some primo weed and didn't share?"

"Ha, no. I'm serious." I lean on the table like a general overlooking a map of the battlefield, only it's merely a laptop and some craft materials Paxton hasn't put away yet. "We have a huge problem of the supernatural kind, and I need your help to fix it."

"Gotcha." Allison gestures toward the archway separating the dining room from the living room. "Okay. Speak freely."

She just did a little magic to keep our conversation private. The girls won't be able to overhear us. Nice. Witches are super handy.

I explain the situation in as much detail as possible, including the power orb, the need to destroy it, and the magical wards protecting it. I leave out the part about me almost being destroyed by such magic. My phrasing is 'got stuck in an unwinnable position and had to get out of there.' This gets a stare from Anthony that totally reminds me of the way Danny used to shoot disappointed looks at the kids whenever he caught them lying. He doesn't say anything. Probably because he knows my lie of omission is for Tammy's emotional benefit.

Predictably, Allison is all 'ooh! Frost nymph!' and can't wait to meet her.

Tammy emits an 'aww' sound.

"She's not a cute little helpless faerie thing," I say, glancing at my daughter. "She's as tall as you are, and fierce. Just... this group of demon cultists seems to have magic specifically designed to attack beings like her."

"Downside to being a potent elemental," says Allie. "Beings of that nature often have an exploitable vulnerability. Creatures highly resistant or immune to cold are usually defenseless against fire-based attacks." As she says this, she closes her eyes. I know the look. It's a sorta eyes-half-closed meditation.

She's looking for her—the frost nymph.

"So, what's our plan?" Tammy leans on the table. "Or should I say, what's *your* plan? I volunteer to stay home and watch the kids."

Surprisingly, my daughter's giving off a mild sense of disappointment. Part of her evidently didn't object to diving headlong into dangerous situations. While she mostly kind of sat back and helped us coordinate things via telepathy, it still hadn't been the safest place for her. Even at her most powerful, she hadn't been physically any tougher, stronger, or faster than an ordinary teenager. Maybe she's relieved at no longer having any reason to go near supernatural problems, but also feels a bit guilty about not being able to be with us and help.

"Yep. You're going to stay here where you're needed the most." I take her hand. "Can't leave the girls home alone."

"She's alive." Allison suddenly opens her eyes. "They've got her stuck inside some kind of giant fireball."

"Still?" I blink. Ugh, that poor nymph. Well, at least she's not dead.

"Yeah." Allie's eyes widen. "And holy cow, that's a mess."

"What did you see?" asks Tammy.

"Umm." Allison gazes into space. "A whole lot of big, white furry monsters. A creepy wooden statue of Azopherith, and a whole bunch of realm noise."

Ant, Kingsley, and Tammy all stare at her as if she'd spoken some crazy foreign language.

"Umm, what?" I ask. "Let's start with what an 'Azopherith' is."

"Demon lord of winter and suffering," mutters Allison. "He's kind of mean. As demons go, he's not particularly dangerous. Ice demons are in the minority, and the fire-based ones always pick on them. This kinda makes them moody. Anyway, Azopherith has had a small cult following among people living in brutally cold areas since before humans learned how to read and write. They think he's the reason it's so intolerably frigid and if they appease him, they'll be allowed to survive."

"You got all that from a giant stick figure?" I blink... and can't help but think of my run-in with Jack Frost recently. Boy, these winter tricksters are kind of assholes.

She nods, then plays innocent. "Well, maybe I had his name pop into my head for no particular reason yesterday while you were napping. Did some research."

"What did your research tell you?" asks Kingsley.

"This guy's bad news. But… he's also super limited." She grins. "He basically can't do much for very long anywhere on Earth the temperature is above like… forty. His power also requires a material conduit."

Tammy squints. "Material conduit?"

"Think of it like a cell phone call. He can't do anything to affect the mortal world unless he has someone here letting him in the door." Allison pretends to hold a phone to her ear. "This Kratos guy is effectively on the phone with his demon boss, getting power from the link. Hang up the phone, break that connection, the demon has no more power to affect the world."

"Until some other jerk makes a deal with him." Anthony frowns.

"Nyali was right then." I reach for my hip—and *don't* draw a sword. Drat. Need water. "Smash the orb and Kratos loses power."

"Power that's being fed to him from the demon, via the orb?" asks Tammy.

"Right," I said. "I think."

"Okay, so what's your plan?" Tammy sets her

hands on her hips.

"Seems obvious enough." Allison grins. "Ant and Kingsley play monkey pong. I'll deal with the demoniacs, and Sam figures out a way to destroy the conduit orb. It's going to have a highly specific vulnerability. It looks like glass, but it's not going to break unless you find the one thing that can do it."

"Already got it covered." I lock stares with Allison and think about the ice blade Nyali gave me. Hopefully, enough of the mental link we once had remains for her to see.

"Nice." She snaps her fingers. "Then we're set. Oh, wait. One thing real quick." Allison rushes to the kitchen and returns with a small bowl containing three ice cubes.

We stand there in bewildered silence for a moment as she sprinkles a bit of sugar, mint oil, and some other green crumbly substance over the cubes. Finally, she holds the bowl out to me and Kingsley.

"Here. Take one each and swallow it whole."

Tammy gags.

"Seriously?" I ask, squirming.

"Yeah. There's a reason not many people do magic or witchcraft." Allison picks up a cube for herself. "It can be weird and uncomfortable sometimes. This spell will keep us warm for a while."

Kingsley's expression is as obvious as the hair on his face. Watching Allison swallow an ice cube whole without flinching has placed certain rude humorous remarks into the tip of his brain that he is not going to speak aloud. At least, he better not, since he's about to eat one as well.

Might as well get this over with.

I pick up a cube, pinching it between two fingers. Before I can think too much about what I'm doing, I gulp it down. Ugh. This has got to be the most uncomfortable thing I've done in quite a long time. No, being impaled on a bloom of giant icicles doesn't count. That was heinously painful, not 'uncomfortable.'

When I stop choking and coughing, I glare at Allison, my right eye open wider than the left. "Why did we have to swallow the darn thing whole?"

"Because chewing ice is bad for your teeth," says Tammy.

Allison points at her. "That's part of it."

I stare.

"Seriously, though." Allison giggles in a 'just kidding' manner. "The ice can't break right now. It's enchanted. It's also going to melt super slow. As long as the ice is in our bellies, we won't be bothered by how cold it gets outside."

"Neat," says Tammy. "Why didn't Ant get one?"

"He won't need it." Allison pats him on the arm.

He nods in a 'that's true' manner.

"How long does this last?" I press a hand to my stomach over a noticeable cold spot.

"About four hours." She scratches idly at her gut.

Tammy cling-hugs my left arm. "You're really going back there after you almost died?"

"How did you know?" I ask.

"The worry in Kingsley's voice when he called us."

One of these days I'll quit trying to protect my kids from everything. Just wanted Tammy to have one less worry tonight. Is that so wrong? I nod and say, "Yeah. This guy intends to kill everyone in that village as a sacrifice to power something huge and demonic." I pat her hand reassuringly. "He's going to reveal the existence of supernatural power to the world, which is ultimately going to lead to nuclear destruction."

"Sounds rough," says Kingsley.

"Didn't you retire from hunting demons?" Anthony nudges me.

"Yeah, but they don't really care about me retiring." I sigh and explain how they ended up using Milo as bait to lure me there. "I'm not making any new enemies, but the ones I made aren't going away just because I want them to leave us alone."

Tammy scratches her head. "I don't remember pissing off an ice demon."

"Azopherith is a mercenary of sorts," says Allison. "When Kratos asked for power, some other demon that Sam pissed off probably paid him to require Kratos attack Sam in exchange for the power."

"Demons have money?" Kingsley scratches his head.

Allison shrugs. "Payment can be anything. Favors, power, not just cash."

"True." Tammy frowns. "If that's the case, maybe you should've kept the sword."

I shake my head. "While it would've made it easier to deal with them, as long as I carried it, more and more demons would keep coming after me until it became overwhelming. Not so terrible if I wandered the earth alone, moving from place to place like Jack Reacher. But living here in Fullerton, with kids and a known address... I'm just asking for trouble. More than I'm willing to deal with."

"All right," says Anthony in a serious way-too-adult tone of voice. "We're going in there to take this guy out?"

"Damn straight," grumbles Kingsley.

"Hang on." I raise a hand at each of them. "If this guy is merely possessed, I'd prefer if we didn't kill him. If he's not possessed and is really an evil prick, then... well... if he survives, he survives. If not, oops."

Allison attempts to sneakily make a 'throat cutting' gesture at Kingsley.

I take this to mean Kratos is not, in fact, possessed but really an evil bastard.

Kingsley's eager smile ought to be reassuring, but it's having the opposite effect. No, I'm not *that* bothered by him wanting to kill the man who damn near killed me. I love that about Kingsley. I'm worried he's going to give into anger as soon as he sees the guy and get careless.

"Are we ready then?" asks Allison.

"I've been ready for the past twenty-six hours," grumbles Kingsley.

"One sec." Anthony runs back to his room. He returns in a moment with his school backpack hastily stuffed with a change of clothes. He hands it to Allison. "Hang onto that for me, please."

He intends, of course, to let the Fire Warrior out.

Something tells me those yetis are not going to like him.

Allison, Kingsley, Anthony, and I link hands around the table.

"All right." I close my eyes and summon the dancing flame. "Please put the tray tables in the upright position and fasten your seatbelts."

Chapter Twenty-four
Werewolf, Witch, Angel, Vampire

Kingsley's contained rage is powerful enough to affect me simply from holding his hand.

I had wanted to aim for a spot in the forest somewhere distant enough from the diabolist's camp to afford us the ability to sneak in. As the dancing flame forms in the blackness of my closed eyes, his fury shoves my aim point right into the middle of the camp. I'm vaguely aware of Allison telepathically screaming about 'don't do it, not in the trees' and something about a boundary layer between worlds.

At the absolute last second, before committing to pulling us through the opening in the fire, I redirect my aim point to wide open snow outside the forest. The sensation is remarkably similar to being on a rollercoaster taking a hairpin turn and loop at the same time—if said rollercoaster happened to be rocket powered.

We appear in the snow... and promptly fall over.

At least I do. Face down, suddenly too sick to move.

A soft "mrmph!" comes from Allison.

Kingsley emits an annoyed grumbling half-growl.

My son grunts faintly, then farts. And... since we're in the Himalayan mountains (near the peaks) it echoes across the countryside. Proof there really is an almost-seventeen-year-old boy in there some-where: he finds this hilarious.

Oh, the valiant charge of heroes we are.

Feels as though someone put my guts on spin cycle. As soon as my insides stop churning around, I push myself up and lift my face from the snow. Allison is embedded head first in the snow a short distance to my left like a human dart, only her legs from the knees up visible, sticking into the air. Like me, Kingsley merely slumped over forward. An-thony's standing by a hole. Judging from the dam-age to the snow, I'm guessing he landed like Alli-son, only went in feet first.

I scramble upright and grab Allison's legs. An-thony hurries over to help and we easily pull her up out of the snow. She looks ill, as if she's about to throw up or just got done doing so. Fortunately, any evidence of sickness is quite well buried.

"Sorry about that," I rasp.

Allison opens her mouth for a split second, then clamps it shut. She raises a hand as if asking for a moment. We all look at her. Over the course of the next fifty seconds or so, the 'I'm gonna be sick' quality to her expression fades away.

"You okay, Allie?" asks Anthony.

"Getting there." She rubs her forehead. "Sam, that wasn't your fault. This forest isn't supposed to be here."

I nod. "Yeah, I figured that out earlier, since it's not on the map."

She gives me this cheesy smile. "Not that I'm any sort of expert on vampire abilities, but teleporting into a space where two different worlds simultaneously exist can have bizarre consequences. I think you basically dodged at the last second before we got ripped apart."

Kingsley raises both eyebrows.

"Well, maybe it would've been just me." Allison rolls her eyes. "You guys are all pretty tough. That last few seconds before we appeared, it felt like I was spinning head over heels."

"Same," says Anthony. "Ma had her wings out to stop the rotation and I think Kingsley was just too angry to surrender to the laws of physics."

I glance at my son. "I had my wings out?"

He nods. "Yeah."

"Strange. I don't remember using them." I dust

snow off myself. "Anyway. Inglorious arrival aside, we should hurry."

Kingsley snarls. In flagrant disregard to Allison's presence, he strips down to nothing but body hair, then hands his suit, shoes, socks, and boxers to Allison to put in the backpack. I swear she's about to pass out. Allie's had a bit of a crush on him for a while. She's staring up at him like some stunned high school nerd girl who just had the star quarterback ask her to prom.

When he shapeshifts into a giant black wolf, the spell breaks… and she starts to blush.

Trying to play it casual, she stuffs his clothes into the pack containing Anthony's spare outfit.

Meanwhile, I know Anthony has a crush on her… and undoubtedly wishes she would look at him like that. Glad she doesn't. I'm sure she's flattered.

Moving on...

We start walking toward the encampment. On the way, I go over the layout and what to expect.

When finished, Allison says, "That giant statue is probably what contains the ward spells. Unless there are other smaller talismans nearby you didn't notice."

"I'll keep my eye out for them," I say.

Kingsley stares at me. I *think* I know what that look means.

"Not far," I say.

He emits an urgent snort type of sound and

shakes his head.

It's really got to be super frustrating as a were-wolf, losing the ability to talk.

"He wants to know what the guy looks like who almost stabbed you," says Allison.

Oh. Oops. And yay for psychics. "The guy with glowing red eyes. Black beard. Tall."

Kingsley the wolf picks up speed, stalking forward faster than we can go in such deep snow. His huge paws are like snowshoes. Uh oh. Big guy's going to get himself in trouble if he rushes in there alone. Speaking of getting into it… I pause walking long enough to reach for the ground and try the ice blade thing again. Within a few seconds of me wanting it to happen, a whole bunch of snow floats into the air and condenses into a luminescent ice blade.

"Ooh, that's pretty," says Allison. "How'd you figure that out?"

A tingle wraps over my brain. Her question immediately made me think of Nyali, and Allison saw the answer in my thoughts right away. My friend is in her forties now, but she still makes the same excited 'ooh' face of a kid. She's definitely going to be one of those 'fun' old ladies in another forty years.

"That's some serious magic, Sam. Like... hardcore fairy magic. If I'm not mistaken, it should last for a long, long time."

"Meaning?"

"You should be able to keep making that ice sword for damn near the rest of your life."

I whistle. The rest of my life could be a very long time indeed.

Meanwhile, since the big furry guy isn't slowing down, the three of us rush after him.

It doesn't take long for the proverbial poop to hit the fan. Mere minutes after we're among the trees, Kingsley launches himself into the air as a black-furred missile. He crashes into a yeti, biting it around the shoulder and neck. After essentially tackling the creature, Kingsley whips it up into the air and smashes it back to the ground amid an explosion of snow. The beast disintegrates into smoke.

His vulgar display of raw physical strength momentarily leaves me staring in disbelief. Whoa. He is *really* angry.

The death wail of the yeti attracts the attention of others.

My son charges forward and does something I have never, ever seen him do before. Hell, didn't know it was even possible. Seriously, WTF? As he runs to Kingsley's aid, my son seems to grow two or three feet. He's seriously about the same size of the yetis himself.

Oh, wait... his skin... it's glowing now.

It's like he's in a partial transformation. Not quite the full Fire Warrior, which easily stands fifteen feet tall.

My heart seriously can't take this.

Beyond the skirmish line, about 200 feet in the distance, the diabolists run out of their shacks. Much to my relief, I spot Nyali apparently still alive, trapped in a ten-foot flame sphere nearest the largest of the rickety buildings.

She, too, has apparently noticed the attack and is standing on her toes trying to get a better view, her expression hopeful.

"Allie," I whisper-shout, "Can you get rid of that big fireball?"

"Umm. I don't know, but I'll try."

At that moment, one of the diabolists throws an ice comet at my son. Panic and rage collide in my heart… until Anthony swats the magical projectile aside with his forearm. Holy shit. Pardon my French.

"One sec," says Allison.

She grabs some kind of dreamcatcher like talisman from her pocket, holds it up, and concentrates. The six visible diabolists appear to abruptly lose the ability to throw ice balls at us. They're waving their arms as if trying to, but nothing happens. Allison's impish grin tells me she's somehow counterspelling them.

Kingsley and Anthony are handling the onslaught of yetis well enough—one ripping out throats and the other driving a fist through faces—but there are just so damn many of them the guys aren't making much in the way of forward progress. They are, however, providing a serious distraction for the diabolists, who have not apparently noticed me or Allison yet.

I sprout my wings and leap into the air, hoping to go over the yeti battle and take on the statue of Azopherith. Seriously don't know how Allison recognized it as anything. It's no more detailed than a massive stick figure with antlers, somewhere between a Burning Man effigy and a freakishly human-shaped random twig found on the forest floor —only it's made from an entire tree trunk.

It's not rooted in place at least. Maybe I can knock it over...

My plans don't quite work out. Again, I crash into an invisible bubble over the statue. This time, I bounce off, catch myself, and study the circle around the shrine. Allison was right. There are some other objects here. They look like glowing blue ice crystals tied to torch-sized sticks embedded in the ground. Right as I look at one, a gathering of energy coalesces around it, takes the form of an ice dagger, and launches itself at my face.

If Anthony can do it, maybe I can too. I attempt to block the projectile… and I do, more or less. I'm not ready for the force, alas. The ice missile smacks into my sword, which then smacks me in the face because I didn't put enough strength behind it. Oof. Annoying, but not painful. Next time, I'll get it.

The diabolists summon another wave of yetis. Allison responds by gesturing in a different manner. Now, the diabolists appear to be ineffectively attempting to summon more yetis. Ha. Good one Allie!

In frustration, one hurls an ice comet at Anthony, which beans him in the back of the head, knocking him a step to the side. This gives a yeti the chance to get past his defenses and pound my son into the snow. Seems like Allie can only stop a specific spell at once… and the diabolists are figuring this out. She starts jockeying back and forth between flushing yeti summonings and making ice comets fizzle. Unfortunately, she can't get all of them, but she's definitely cutting down their effectiveness.

As soon as my son disappears from sight beneath a pile of white furry creatures, my sense of self-preservation evaporates. I lose track of what everyone else is doing and see red. The statue can wait. I flap my wings hard, throwing myself forward at the spot where my son is buried.

My sword pierces to the hilt in the back of the nearest back. The force of my dive knocks the huge beast flat on its chest for a second before it evaporates. Right as I recover my balance and stand up, a great blast of flames erupts from the ground behind me.

I spin around as the Fire Warrior rises out of a cloud of fog, giving off a low, annoyed growl.

He's standing in a three-foot-deep crater where the snow has ceased existing. Dark brown dirt that likely hasn't seen daylight for centuries forms a large circle around his feet, steam wafting up from the baking earth.

All the yeti practically scream and scramble over themselves to run away. It's as if a man in a Hollywood quality devil costume just jumped out of a box in the middle of a kindergarten classroom.

Kingsley is absolutely content to allow the yetis to flee. Now, there's nothing between him and the diabolists. He bolts after the nearest man, who's too frustrated trying to figure out why his magic isn't working right to notice the wolf until it's too late.

Crunch.

Anthony grabs a fleeing yeti by a fistful of its fur, swings it around, and throws the creature at the giant statue. The yeti smashes into the primitive depiction of the demon lord of winter with so much force it disintegrates to smoke on contact... knocking the statue into a backward lean.

Hmm. Hang on a second. No stupid force bubble thing. Kratos must have forgotten to re-cast it after I left. Or maybe it requires some bizarre magical component he doesn't have more of. Whatever. It's gone. I glance at the Fire Warrior mopping up stray yetis with ease. Yeah, my boy can take care of himself. He's not in any danger right now.

I run-fly-zoom back toward the statue, feeling much like a fighter jet trying to dive attack an anti-aircraft battery. Dozens of ice daggers fly at me from the little crystal talisman things I'm flying straight at. I roll, twist, and swerve side to side. A few score glancing blows on my shoulder, leg, and left hip.

At the last second, before crashing into the statue, I swing myself around and plant my feet on the wood above and below the cavity containing the big orb. Despite its significant backward lean, the force of me hitting the statue barely moves it. For a mere second or so, I defy gravity and stand sideways while stabbing my ice blade at the orb.

The tip bounces off with a *click*, failing to break through. It does, however, scratch it. Better, it knocks the basketball-sized crystal ball loose from whatever force kept it in the hollow. My momentum equalizes with gravity, removing my ability to 'stand' sideways on the tree trunk. Before I fall, I spring away, flip over, and land on my feet. The orb's plopped to the ground not far from the statue's base.

Nice.

I walk the three steps over to it and raise my ice sword in both hands for the smashing blow.

… and my warning sense screams bloody murder.

"Samantha, be wary!" shouts Nyali.

I'm already spinning around when she yells, but I appreciate the attempt. Kratos—or a being made entirely of white snow in the general shape of Kratos—is right behind me, that wicked single-edged dagger poised to have gone into my back.

The expression of shock on his face at me suddenly spinning around and parrying his thrust is epic. I damn near swat the blade out of his grip. He staggers to his right, barely managing to compensate for the force I put into my defense. Like a serpent shedding a second skin made of thick eggshell, the whiteness coating his entire body breaks apart and flakes off. Really him, not a snow clone. Just a... camouflage spell of some kind. Wearing a thick, grey parka.

"Little different when I can move, huh?" I narrow my eyes at him.

He waves his arms around—not sure if it's for balance or he's casting a spell, snarling at me. The instant my alarm sense screams, it's pretty obvious he's doing a spell. I flap my wings and launch myself straight up. The same icicle bloom he impaled me on last time erupts from the ground beneath me. One spire jabs me in the back of the right leg, drawing blood, but I mostly stand on it and use its rapid eruption as a catapult to launch me into the sky.

Ow. That stings, but a small gash on my leg is *way* better than being impaled by crisscrossing ice lances.

At the apex of my ascent, I grab my ice sword in two hands and tilt over into a diving attack... but before I can even start dropping on Kratos, a black flash smothers him. Uh oh. Kingsley found him. A tangle of parka-covered limbs, werewolf fur, snarling, and flying drool goes scooting off to the side.

Kratos screams in agony and panic. "Azopherith!"

Kingsley the wolf flips the man into the air, thrashing his body back and forth.

The head diabolist continues shrieking and screaming, now in some other language.

Okay, well… that's taken care of. I spin and come face to face with a twelve-foot-tall sculpture of really pointy icicles, once meant to impale me. Yeah, no thank you. After stepping around the painful mess, I jog over to the orb that's causing all these problems.

I should probably say something witty, but I'm not Arnold Schwarzenegger, so I simply barbarian smash my ice sword into the orb.

The formerly glowing-blue glasslike orb instantly turns opaque coal black, then cracks in half, throwing off a bunch of sparks and smoking crystalline fragments. All fifty or sixty remaining yetis in sight disintegrate at once. Nyali's prison of fire also dissipates.

Nice.

I turn to share a victory smile with Kingsley—only to discover he's a lot closer than I expected. As in, he's flying at me. My brain has just enough time to process the idea the enormous black thing about to crash into me is Kingsley before we collide.

He might be close to a thousand pounds of werewolf, but it's really like getting walloped with a dense pillow. Most of that is me being supernaturally tough. Some is him being soft. Some is the snow we land on.

Kingsley rolls off me right away, shaking his head in disorientation.

Sprawled on the ground beside him, I peer up at where he came from and my stomach sinks.

I've locked stares with a ten-foot-tall blue skinned apparition that's in no way even close to being human. He's evidently male, and not terribly buff. Kinda skinny actually. Elongated arms dangle on either side of his body, so spindly they resemble the gnarled branches of a tree. He's wearing a robe-like garment with fancy ice crystal shoulder pads and one of those medieval hood-coif deals that covers his entire head except for his face. Black eyes, black teeth, horns, and two giant antler-like things sticking out to either side of his head. I can't tell if the antlers are actually his or part of his icy crown.

"Oh, shit," I mutter. "It's the ice demon."

Chapter Twenty-five
Chill Out

Most people, when they think of demons, imagine either these big monstrous creatures or super buff dudes with black wings.

Azopherith is neither of those. He's tall but rail thin and kinda wizard-like. Guess that part makes sense given all the magical powers he gave his cultish followers. Still, he is a demon… and he's looking at me in a not-nice way. If the glower on his face is any indication, he wants to skin me alive, upholster a new chair with my hide, then sip wine out of my skull while watching scarab beetles devour the rest of my corpse he's keeping alive with magical means so I can enjoy the feeling of being gnawed upon.

That was needlessly detailed and graphic, says Allison's voice in my head.

Her telepathy is a reminder that she still has the ability, even if I don't. Maybe also that we have a deeper connection than most, since she used to drink blood from me. (Sounds gross, I know, but it was just a little bit from my finger, nothing *too* weird.) Anyway, I know she can't use her telepathy with just anyone. But as a powerful witch, the ability is there for her to cultivate. Much the same way Elizabeth cultivated it originally, back in the day. That said, I can only speak to her when she appears in my thoughts, not the other way around. Meaning, unless she establishes a connection, I can't reach out to her... or her mind. Or anyone's mind, for that matter. For the best, but it sure came in handy at times.

Yeah, but, look at him. I glance in her direction while gesturing at the demon. He's *that* angry.

I drag myself upright. The wound in my leg isn't making me any faster. Ugh, this is going to suck.

Kingsley darts protectively in front of me, which appears to amuse the demon. Azopherith tilts his oversized head the way a human might regard a puppy doing something cute.

Hmm. Not sure an ice blade is the best weapon to use against an ice demon, but it might be a paradox. It worked on his orb, right? Whatever he has planned is going to hurt. Like, a lot.

An amber-orange bolt of energy streaks in from the side and hits the demon in the chest.

Azopherith glances down at the spot, then at Allison. His expression is pure 'were you expecting that to do something, mortal?'

"Oh, shit." She gasps and ducks behind a tree.

The demon steps toward us.

Kingsley growls louder.

Anthony, presently the Fire Warrior, strolls up behind Azopherith, great flaming wings spreading outward from his back. Another new trick for Ant. Makes sense... angels and wings. Still, hadn't seen these before.

Wicked cool.

Weirdly, the demon doesn't notice the Fire Warrior getting closer. Oh, he's so damn angry with me for ruining his plans, he's pulling a Kingsley.

Meanwhile, dark blue energy coalesces in the demon's hand, likely some manner of awfulness he's about to throw at me.

I point. "Might want to look behind you."

Naturally, he ignores me, thinking it's a trick. The instant his hand twitches, Kingsley leaps, grabbing the wrist in his jaws... just as a spray of intense cold and thousands of tiny needles wash over me amid a blinding flash.

Next thing I know, I'm flat on the ground again with at least twenty icicles pinned through me. I feel like a dead frog in biology class. Kingsley's on his side, not far away, snarl-gasping. Something— smoke or magical energy—wisps up from his fur making him look as if he'd been hit with a massively powerful electrical shock. Dammit. I'm really getting tired of being impaled with icicles.

The Fire Warrior appears highly displeased at what's happened to me. He taps the demon on the shoulder.

Azopherith's frosty eyebrows notch upward. I imagine he's rather surprised I wasn't lying about there being something behind him. He twists to peer back over his shoulder.

In a roar of angry flames, Anthony's huge fist plows into the demon's face, crushing its entire head down into its torso, which also breaks apart into a swirling cloud of blue light and ice fragments. The fabric of his 'robe' appears to freeze in an instant and also shatter into spinning shards.

Anthony regards the rapidly melting pieces of demon, then nods slowly.

All the ice needles pinning me to the ground disintegrate.

Even though I could theoretically get up now, I don't. Whatever it did to me had likely been intended to hold me in place rather than do a lot of damage. Still, it hurts. Won't take *too* long for the wounds to close.

Allison emerges from behind her hiding tree, near to cackling with laughter. Thanks to our mental link, I know she found it hilarious how Anthony just smashed the demon like a kid stepping on an empty soda can. She and I both had been expecting a long, painful battle. Not going to complain, though.

Sometimes rock, paper, scissors is better.

Ice demon, meet fire angel.

Nyali zooms over and helps me up. "You returned."

"Yep. Sorry for leaving you like that." I rub my side where an icicle pierced. "Didn't have a choice. Needed to *poof* when I did, or we both would've been dead."

She presses her forehead to mine. "I understand."

Allison trudges across the snow to me. Kingsley groans and lifts himself up to stand, swaying on his feet.

A sickly groan emits from Kratos.

We all turn to look at him. The diabolist, somehow still alive, lays on the snow in a twisted heap. His parka and fur leggings appear to have absorbed much of the damage Kingsley's teeth inflicted. Dude's still a mess, though.

"His eyes aren't glowing red anymore," I say.

Nyali shakes her head at him. "The foolish human welcomed the demon to reside within him."

I bite my lip. "What do we do with him? I don't think the police will arrest a guy for 'malicious summoning with intent for world domination.'"

"No…" Allison rolls her eyes. "They'd put *us* away in a mental hospital for even trying to tell them about it."

"He is no longer any threat," says Nyali.

The Fire Warrior shrinks back down into Anthony. Allison tosses him the backpack, which he promptly opens. We all look away as he dresses.

"Can't he just start worshiping the demon again?" I ask.

"Nah." Anthony shakes his head. "He failed Azopherith. The demon will either ignore him or kill him if he dares to try to make contact again."

Allison glances at him, peeking through her fingers to make sure he's dressed. He is. "Wait. Didn't you kill the demon?"

"No. I just sent it back where it belongs." Anthony pulls a sweater on. "Demons cannot be killed in this world... unless with the Devil Killer. Otherwise, we're only destroying their physical manifestation. But... it'll be a century or two before Azopherith can manifest here again. If we wanted to kill him permanently, we'd have to go to whatever demiplane he lives on natively. I'm game if you are."

"Hard pass. I think it's a little colder there than even this place." I gaze around.

"Probably." Anthony sits and pulls his socks on.

I look around at the now-deserted camp. No sign of the diabolists except for two or three lumps that might be corpses thanks to Kingsley. The yetis are no more. The ward talismans around the statue appear to be non-magical now. Great. We are done. I let my ice sword collapse into a splash of water.

"Aww." Allison fake pouts. "Why'd you do that? It was pretty."

"It's not gone, just put away. I can re-make it whenever I want… just need water."

"Neat," says Anthony. "Where'd you get it from?"

I gesture at Nyali. "She taught me a new trick."

The frost nymph bows at me. "You have saved not only my existence but that of my kind, this village of humans, and much of your world. We are eternally grateful."

"Happy to help." I rub my jaw. Feeling like I got run over by a spiked steamroller made of ice is making me want to spend the next two hours soaking in a hot bath.

Kingsley shifts back to human form. Anthony tosses over the backpack of clothing. Which gets me wondering how the clothing of two huge males could fit in a simple backpack.

A little packing magic, says Allie in my mind.

When the big guy is dressed, Anthony slings the backpack over his left shoulder. "Home then? Before Tammy and Pax get too worried?"

"Yeah. I think I have enough oomph left in me for one more teleport." I hold my hands out to either side. "I will, however, be spending the rest of the afternoon relaxing in the tub."

Kingsley sidles up next to me, mostly dressed, though he didn't button his shirt yet. "I have a hot tub."

I lean against him. "Your temptations are… effective."

Chapter Twenty-six
Strangely Normal

Spending an entire night at Kingsley's, mostly in the spa, was the perfect cure.

I've almost forgotten about being impaled and frozen. Last I heard from the Boone family, they'd decided to list the house for sale and return to Ohio as soon as they have a buyer. Considering the differential in real estate between here and there, I'm guessing they're going to end up with a place of comparable size and some money in the bank.

Still don't know if the grandparents were real or all just a fabrication of the demons. Kaitlyn seems to believe the house really did belong to her parents, so perhaps all the demon did was hasten her mother's death so they'd inherit the house. Or maybe it only decided to mess with me by saying that. It's not like the demon would have needed to specifically lure Milo Boone to California to bait me. I'd run off like an idiot to save any child in danger.

It's foolish to try to understand why demons do anything. They're more chaotic and random than two-year-olds hopped up on sugar.

Two days have passed since the fight with Kratos. Two wonderfully normal days spending time with my family... and banging my head against a wall in regard to Sherbet's case. I'm still in the post 'we just did some crazy supernatural stuff' winding down state, so I'm working from home today. Not ready for the office.

Tammy meanders in from school a little after one in the afternoon. Did I mention she has early days as a senior? Her last period class is a study hall, so she's allowed to go home since she's eighteen and has a license. More academically motivated students would've stuffed an AP class in that schedule spot instead of a blank period, but hey... not everyone needs to finish college a year early, right? All this weird stuff I've seen kinda puts things in perspective. People need to do whatever makes them happy, not follow the formula society dictates is proper. College, trade school, none of the above, whatever. Except for immortals like me, people keep going around and around. No sense trying to rush and get everything done in one lifetime.

"Hey, Ma." She sets her backpack down on the

dining room table and flops in a chair, looking at me over the screen of my laptop.

"Hey, kiddo. How was your day?"

"Fine. Only a few months left until graduation. Feels weird." She scrunches her nose. "Like, I simultaneously can't wait to be free from school, but it's also kinda scary."

"Scary how?" I shift my gaze off the screen to her.

"My whole life has been basically school so far. I'm not going to know how to handle having so much time to myself."

I laugh.

"What?" She squints at me.

"Time to yourself." I cackle. "That's hilarious."

She folds her arms. "What are you talking about?"

"When I was your age, I used to think school was such a burden... then I got a job." I wink. "Like, a real job. Not working for my mother. Try getting home at closer to six every day."

"Ugh." She facepalms. "What am I doing? Quick, get Allison to do something to make me into a kid again. Screw the forty-hour week."

"You'll be fine. You have energy. You're not supposed to want to be a kid again until you're past forty and overwhelmed."

She holds up both hands. "The trick there is not to let yourself get overwhelmed. I shall be happy in my free-spirited mediocrity. Why run myself ragged for 'success' or whatever?"

"As long as you're happy and not out on the streets."

"You'd never let me end up on the streets." She grins. "Besides, I'm probably going to live with you forever. Good luck getting me out of here."

"Okay," I say, not minding the idea at all, even though I know she's probably teasing me.

She twirls a lock of hair around her finger. "Or, I might run into some guy twice my age with a house van and spend the next ten years going across the country with him."

"Sounds delightful," I say, not taking the bait.

"Aww, you're no fun." She sticks her tongue out at me. "Oh, speaking of not fun... I still haven't been able to find anything about that Aladdin thing."

"Damn."

She leans forward, elbows on the table, chin on her hands. "Yeah. The place it came from is either so old it's gone or it never went on the internet."

"Right. That's the problem." I cut my gaze over to my phone. Need to call Fang again, see if he's heard anything. Can't yet. He won't be awake now.

"Oh, Ant said you got a sword again."

"Yeah."

"Can I see it?"

I look around, shrug. "Sure, why not...?"

We go to the kitchen. I turn on the water at the sink, then concentrate on it the same way I did the snow. The stream bends upward in defiance of gravity and begins to glow a soft blue. Soon, it forms into the icy longsword... and the remaining water from the tap flows normally into the drain again. A faint squealing, crackling noise comes from the blade as it condenses. Here, back in California where it's considerably warmer than the Himalayas, the sword gives off a constant aura of fog... like dry ice.

"Wow." Tammy stares at the blade for a moment before gingerly touching one finger to it. "It's cold."

"Ice."

"Won't it break?" She tilts her head.

"It can, but it's magical... and I can always make a new one."

"New one?" She blinks.

"Yeah, this sword isn't a one-time deal. I don't like keep it in an interdimensional scabbard. If it breaks, I can summon it again, and it will reappear whole again. Or I can just make another one from more water. Pretty sure, though, I can only make one at a time, though that might be interesting to experiment with. Anyway, it's a conjuration of sorts. Not real for very long."

"Then, what... it melts back to water?"

"Something like that."

She nods. "Wow. So much for our life being normal, huh?"

"Yeah..." I hold the sword up, smiling at it.

"You know, it kinda makes me feel normal to have a sword again. I missed it."

"Hah. Ma, you sound like Viggo."

I raise an eyebrow at her. "Viggo? Who's that? New boyfriend?"

She fans herself. "I wish. I'm talking about the guy who played Aragorn in the *Lord of the Rings* movies. Someone interviewed him and he said something about how he'd been carrying a sword around all day for so long it felt weird not to have one."

Oh. Viggo Mortensen. I allow myself a little fantasy there as well. Then glance at my daughter. "Hey, stop thinking about him like that. He's old enough to be your father."

She rolls her eyes at me. Her expression is totally 'I'm eighteen, I can do what I want,' but she says nothing.

By simply deciding I don't need the sword now, the dang thing drops into a splash on my kitchen floor. My daughter and I grab some paper towels and wipe it. Yeah, definitely feels weird wiping up what I know had been a super strong sword.

We resume going about our ordinary day. Still have that process to serve, too. It's going to be tricky. Just need to wait the guy out until he feels secure enough to go home or out in public. Timing is key there.

Before long, I run out to pick up Paxton and Renae from school. I savor being Mom for the remainder of the afternoon through dinner.

Fang calls about an hour after sunset. He must have sensed me thinking about him.

"Please have good news," I say by way of answering.

"Hello there, Moon Dance." He chuckles. "I do. Though, can't say exactly how good it may be. That's up to you. Word is there's a relatively new vampire out there. Not hearing much about who turned her. The feeling I'm getting is she's less than two months old and probably an accident. Sire didn't stick around to show her the ropes."

I groan. "Any idea where this woman is?"

"One guy said something about a Genie Motel."

"Genie Motel, you say?" I stop breathing. Then again, I might have not been breathing the past ten minutes. Honestly, who knows?

Tammy stares at me for two seconds, makes an 'on it' face, then runs to get her laptop out of her backpack.

"Yeah," says Fang. "It's a real dive over in Cerritos. Think it's on Edwards Road."

"Guessing they don't have a website?"

He laughs. "Nope. Doubt they'd advertise much until it becomes legal to sell heroin."

I cringe. "Oh… *that* kind of dive."

"Yeah." Fang emits a wheezy snicker. "People who stay there tend to rent rooms by the month, not the day."

"Thanks, Fang. Gonna go see if I can find her."

"Hey, Sam…" He pauses. "If you do make contact, give her my card. Not good for any of us vamps having a wild one out there. Someone's gotta lead her the right way and all."

"You volunteering?" I raise an eyebrow.

"If not me, I'll set her up with someone."

Heh. Well, at least I know Fang enough to trust he's not interested in her for any unseemly reason. No, all his unseemliness in that regard is firmly directed at me. He, like most undead vampires, is rather pointedly worried about hunters. A new, untrained vampire running around leaving a trail of bodies is bad news for everyone.

"Okay. I'll send her your way."

"Sounds good. Happy hunting."

"Right." I hang up, look at Tammy. "Gotta run out for a bit."

She nods. "Want company?"

"Normally, I'd say sure, but I'm going to a place you'd probably want to avoid."

"You're going to a KISS concert?"

Hah. "No… a dive motel likely full of druggies."

She winces, still all too aware of that alternate dimension version of herself where I died, and she turned to drugs. "Seeing other people doing stupid things doesn't get to me… just as long as I don't have to see myself doing it."

I hug her. She squeezes me back extra hard, as if to apologize for something she never even did. Neither one of us know if what that alternate Tammy did is proof *my* Tammy would make the same choices in the same situation, but she's acting as guilty as if she would… and did.

"Hey," I say in a near whisper. "Don't get all torn up over what-ifs."

"Thanks for not dying," she mumbles into my shoulder.

I wait the few seconds for her to realize that, technically, I *did* die that night in Hillcrest Park. As soon as it hits her, she makes an 'oops' face at me.

"I did, but… thankfully, I got better."

This gets her smiling. "Thank God."

"Okay, Tam-Tam. I'll be back as soon as I can. You're the adult in the house until I return."

"We're screwed," calls Renae from the living room.

Tammy pantomimes rolling up her sleeves. "Did you guys finish your homework yet?"

"Uh oh," whispers Paxton. "See what you did?"

Hah.

"Relax," says Tammy. "I'm going with Mom. Anthony's in charge 'til we get back."

The girls cheer.

"You sure?" I ask.

She shrugs. "Hey, I can at least be an extra set of eyes for you."

Chapter Twenty-seven
Vampire Adrift

Considering it's not the smartest thing for me to keep showing people I can teleport, we use a slightly more conventional means of transportation: the Momvan.

Tammy didn't find anything about the place on the internet other than a few links to news articles about police activity here. As these sorts of places go, it's somewhat tame. Not too much violence, merely a lot of users hanging out there. The cops show up every so often to check for underage runaways or dealers, but for the most part, it looks like they leave them alone. Either that or the news doesn't bother covering it all that much.

The Genie Motel is a fairly small building near the edge of the commercial district in Cerritos. It's at the south end of Edwards Road, in sight of the residential area south of Artesia Boulevard. The area *looks* nice. Even the building doesn't give off the sense of being a 'roach motel' for drug users. Then again, we *are* in California. Even the addicts are glamorous.

I park on the street a reasonable distance from the address. For reasons known only to my subconscious, it seemed like a bad idea to drive right up to it. Maybe I'm merely being self-conscious, not wanting anyone to see me driving to a place like this.

Within seconds of us setting foot on the property, a set of blacked-out windows draws my attention to one room in particular. Someone appears to have taped trash bags to the inside of the glass. Okay, that's a big red—or in this case black—flag.

"Hmm," whispers Tammy, eyeing about a dozen people milling around the area. "Not what I was expecting."

Indeed, this motel reminds me of the art college my brother went to. The campus was so small it didn't have dorms. They rented a whole wing of a motel like this and put the students four to a room there. Teens would hang out in front of the building, doors open, listening to music, drinking beer—if they could get it—and so on.

I make my way over to the room, then knock. Tammy stands behind me a little to the left. Can't say what made her want to come with me or what made me think bringing her was a good idea. Maybe having two women come to talk will make this new vampire feel safer. Not like Tammy can really do much to help me deal with an angry undead. I think she just wants to 'do stuff with mom.' I like having her with me, too, as long as it isn't too dangerous.

Not sure what this qualifies as yet.

The door opens.

A skinny blonde woman in an oversized T-shirt stares quizzically at me. She's barefoot, a little shorter than me, and could be anywhere from sixteen to twenty years old. Sounds from a television fill from the room behind her. I don't smell anything unusual: drugs, dead body, or unknown chemicals.

If I had to ascribe any emotion to her persona at the moment, it would be fear, sadness, loneliness, and a sort of wild abandon. Like an 'if I'm going down, you're all coming with me' vibe. She's not staring at me as if she expects a fight, more as though she's trying to remember if she knows me.

There's a feralness to her presence as well. It's part new vampire, part whatever sort of life she led before ending up one. Her lack of aura is a damn clear indication she's the vampire I've been looking for. Her toes tense, gripping the floor. The beginnings of a fight-or-flight reaction show in her features. Likely, she notes my lack of an aura, too. That is, if she knows what that even means.

"Relax." I hold up a hand. "I'm a friend. Here to help. I know what's happened to you and what you've become."

"Who are you?" asks the girl, a mild hint of a possibly Russian accent in her voice.

"I'm Sam. This is my daughter, Tammy."

The girl eyes Tammy, then me, and says, "She is not like me. You are not like me, either... but you are not, ah... normal, either."

"Nope. I'm special." I smile. "I'm only here to talk and offer whatever help I can. Might be a good idea if we go inside for some privacy."

She again looks at Tammy, then me. I expect hesitation, but she turns with a rather blasé indifference and walks into the room, leaving the door open. Okay, this could mean she's feeling superhuman and not threatened by a pair of women... or she's given up and no longer cares what happens to her.

We step inside. Tammy eases the door closed behind us.

"What is it you think I am?" asks the girl, arms folded, her back still facing us.

"A vampire," I say, matter-of-factly.

"Such things are not real," she says, but sounds less confident.

"Oh, they are. Trust me. I used to be one."

She spins to stare at me, fangs visible, mouth agape in awe. "Used to? There is a way to fix?" She sounds very Russian now, words and sounds forming deep in her throat.

I cringe. "I'm still a vampire of sorts. What happened to me is a once in a billion confluence of crazy circumstances. There's no going back to being a normal human. Not for you, not for me."

"Oh." She stares down. "Why are you here, then?"

"The cops found a dead guy in Fullerton. A teacher, left near a school." I set my hands on my hips. "I've got a fairly good suspicion it might have been your work."

She sits on the edge of the bed. "I do not know what you are speaking about."

"It's okay," says Tammy gently. "The police aren't going to arrest a vampire. Mom's not here to like 'bring you in' or something."

"The body had fang marks on the neck," I say. "Based on their spacing, they'd be about perfect for a woman your size. Whoever killed the teacher also clawed the hell out of him, but in a random, shallow, frenzied way that tells me they were out of their mind at the time. Pure hunger panic."

"I… maybe…" She looks down at her hands. "Do not remember doing it, but there was a dead man next to me when I..." she searches for a word or words, and settles on "woke up."

I sit beside her on the bed. "It really is okay. Well, not for the dead guy, but you didn't mean to do it."

She looks me in the eye.

I explain the 'feeding crazies,' and how vampires can lose their minds if they go too long without having blood. This young woman hasn't quite accepted having become a vampire—or that vampires are real. She eventually becomes comfortable enough to share her name, Rosannah Fedor. In between me explaining what I can remember of being a 'traditional' vampire, she shares a little bit about how she ended up in California. Turns out, she *is* Russian and is not only dealing with the sudden upheaval of becoming an undead, she's struggling to cope with being in a country she doesn't know or understand.

Poor girl was trafficked here… lured by a promise of work that turned out to be high-priced prostitution. I'm much relieved to hear she's older than she looks. Rosannah is twenty years old. When she admits her age, Tammy's eyebrows go up in disbelief. We sit there in stunned, sad silence as this woman explains coming to the US, expecting to work cleaning houses or doing secretary type stuff… only to be brought to an expensive hotel and told to have sex with some rich, powerful guy she'd never seen before and who had to be double her age.

According to her, she tried to nope out of there, but her 'bodyguard' grabbed her and threatened to kill her if she attempted to leave. She goes on to tell us that unbeknownst to the traffickers, the 'client' didn't want her for sex… but rather a blood meal.

Details are a little fuzzy since she doesn't recall the night too much beyond the bodyguard throwing her against the wall when she tried to run away. However, it sounds like the vampire became angry watching this guy slap her around, so he killed the guy. Perhaps his fury got the better of him and he drank too much blood from Rosannah... or something. She describes regaining consciousness in the hotel room beside the corpse of the 'bodyguard' but couldn't move.

Next thing she knew, she woke up in a morgue... and ran away.

"Oh, wow," says Tammy in a whispery voice. "I'm so sorry... That's..."

Rosannah shrugs one shoulder. "I cannot say my situation back home would have been much better. At least I am in America now, and not afraid of those men. They think I am dead. If they find me, I will make *them* dead."

I wince. "While you can easily do that... and maybe should, you will need to be careful about it."

"Why?" She scoffs. "If I am vampire, what do I care about laws or police?"

Tammy whistles. "She really is new."

"Hunters." I exhale. "There are people out there who hunt vampires... and they are dangerous."

Rosannah stares at me while I explain about vampire hunters having almost supernatural abilities and are not merely 'just humans with crossbows.' When I finish, she scowls to the side. "You are telling me I am still weak?"

"No. Not at all. Hunters are very uncommon. All I'm saying is be careful." I gaze around at the room. "Got a friend who is also a vampire like you. He's been around for a while and offered to help you adjust."

"Fang's not a bad guy." Tammy smiles. "Little odd, but what vampire isn't? Besides, his bar is *way* nicer than this place. Kind of out in the open and obvious here. Especially with the blacked-out windows."

I pull the keychain out of my purse. "I think you dropped this."

"Oh, wow." Rosannah reaches for the Hello Kitty figurine. "How did you find?"

"At the second body." I let her take the keys. "I know you didn't kill *that* guy... or the third."

She shakes her head. "No. I saw a man take the body from his car and put it on ground. It was strange."

"You mean stranger than someone dumping a dead guy?" asks Tammy.

"Well... this man." Rosannah scrunches her nose. "I saw the same man the night I went out of my mind. I was kneeling there in the grass beside the dead one, and this man walked up to us. I remember being uneasy. He did not react the way you might think one would react to seeing such a scene." She peers at her hands. "I am sure he saw my claws. Maybe fangs. And of course, he saw the dead man. He did not seem frightened. The way he stared at me, is like little boy finding shiny rock."

Tammy and I exchange a glance.

"Copycat," we say at the same time.

"Cat?" asks Rosannah. "No, cat. Just me. Or"—she holds up her keychain—"Do you mean the Hello Kitty?"

I stifle the urge to chuckle. "No, copycat as in I think the man you saw became fascinated with vampires and has decided to go on a killing spree pretending to be one."

She gasps. "Why?"

"There's the million-dollar question," says Tammy. "Probably just a psycho."

"I think so." Rosanna stares into space, shudders. "He made awful faces, like watching me rip and bite the man got him excited in maybe a sexual way."

"Ewww." Tammy cringes. "Brain bleach please. Mom, make me forget that."

"I can't, Tam-Tam. You know that." Sigh. "Besides, it might not be sexual—just the rush a serial killer gets from the kill. The bodies don't have any evidence they were... *bothered* in any unseemly ways beyond being killed. What did this guy look like?"

Rosannah sits back and begins to brush her long hair. Swear this girl looks like a Barbie doll brought to life. She's supermodel pretty and so thin. No wonder those creeps targeted her. "Man. Late thirties. Hair short. Black. Round cheeks. Lines." She traces her index fingers around her mouth.

Tammy snickers.

Rosannah and I both stare at her.

"What's so funny?" I ask.

"He's got deep lines around his mouth?" Tammy cups her hands around her face like she's about to shout. "There's a teacher like that at my school with really deep creases around his mouth like that. We all tease him that everything he says is in parenthesis."

Ugh. Nerd jokes.

Rosannah appears to have missed the humor. She stares confusedly at Tammy for a moment before shifting her gaze to me. "He drive big blue car. Old. Much bigger than cars now."

"Okay. That's something, at least." Not much, but something.

"C'mon. Grab your things. I'll take you to meet Fang."

She blinks. "His name is Fang? A vampire who calls himself Fang?" She appears on the verge of laughing.

"Yeah. He's had a thing for teeth ever since he was mortal." I grin. "He's a good guy. You'll be safe with him."

"Safer than this place," deadpans Tammy.

"This place is not safe." Rosannah stands.

"I know. That's what I mean." Tammy flails her arms. "C'mon. I wanna get out of here."

Rosannah hurriedly packs up a bunch of clothing, transferring it from the floor to a huge handbag still with the price tags on it. Oh, someone's been a naughty little shoplifter, apparently. Can't really blame her too much. Becoming a vampire is enough of a shock without being stranded in an unfamiliar country with no family, no friends, and no money...

Yeah, she does need some help, if only to keep her urges under control before too many corpses draw hunters like flies.

Chapter Twenty-eight
Trying to Unwind

I'm draped partially over my dining room table, half napping.

It's a little after ten in the morning the following day. Rosannah and Fang hit it off fairly well, damn near throwing off sibling vibes within minutes of meeting. He's totally adopting her like a stray kitten. He's good like that.

I got to bed late and had to fight off the urge to wake my kids up to hug them before crashing. Sitting for hours at Fang's club listening to Rosannah talk about her crummy home life in Russia was a hell of a downer. Her parents remind me of mine. Not overtly abusive, just super neglectful. They barely noticed they had a daughter and two sons living in the apartment with them beyond cooking enough food for everyone.

Made me super grateful to have what I have.

Anyway… I woke up to a long email from Allison replying to my email where I gave her the details of Rosannah's description of the killer. Seems the 'old as hell blue car' might've been the key—well that and a few pieces of the dead guy's personal effects I borrowed from the evidence room. Items in physical contact with a person at the moment they are murdered often pick up on psychic imprints.

Yes, I will return the items. There's a difference between borrowing and stealing.

Allie got a vision of a small house in the suburbs. Even got something of a street name. Starts with B ends with 'wood.' Brentwood, Boxwood, Beechwood, something like that. Between a partial street name and giant old blue car, Sherbet has something to work with.

I just got off the phone with him, giving him the details plus the description of the guy. Fingers crossed he's able to find something. We won't be able to use any supernatural claims in front of a judge.

I suppose it's possible Rosannah could end up serving as a witness to say she observed the guy dumping a body. That doesn't in any way hinge on her being a vampire. Though, if she's introduced to the process, the killer might claim to have seen *her* kill a guy as a vampire. That's either going to blow up into a circus or result in the guy getting put away for being insane. Despite there being no chance the court would take his accusations of her being a vampire seriously, it's a can of worms I'm afraid to open. So, yeah. If I have anything to say about it, Rosannah won't be involved directly anymore.

For a couple hours, I do housework while listening to *Judge Judy* reruns in the background. Kingsley sends me a text to remind me of our rescheduled dinner date. Kinda missed the last one due to being incapacitated. He wants to take me to this fancy place Friday night. Fine with me. I'm not one of those women who demands luxury, but I won't say no to it in small doses. My ordinary little house here is all the extravagance I need.

Tammy walks in from school a little after one. "Hey, Ma. Hungry?"

"Normal hungry or energy hungry?"

"Normal hungry." She grins. "Or both."

I wink. "I could eat."

"Wanna go grab something? I forgot to eat lunch today."

I blink at her. "How do you *forget* to eat lunch when you've got an entire class period dedicated to it?"

"It's… complicated."

I raise both eyebrows. "Boy complicated?"

"Gah. No." She flails. "Why are you so obsessed with me and boys?"

"I'm not obsessed. I just remember being your

age. 'Complicated' usually means embarrassing things you can't talk about with the parents."

She laughs. "Okay. Almost right. It's embarrassing. I'm not doing great in math, so I was getting some extra help."

"That's complicated?" I grab my bag and start for the door, still not sure where we're going for food other than somewhere other than home.

"I decided to ask this girl Grace for help. She's kind of a nerd. No one ever really talks to her." Tammy sighs. "She likes a lot of the same sorts of movies and music I do. We talked about random crap way more than math. But, yeah... I need help with math. Like I said, embarrassing."

"Math isn't easy for some of us."

"Tell me about it."

The tone of her conversation makes it quite obvious this girl is nothing more than a friend. This isn't another Paxton situation. Poor Tammy. She hasn't been spending enough time with her friends lately and I think she's kinda desperate for time hanging out with kids her age. Her usual friends have been busy with after school jobs and such.

We hop in the Prius and she starts driving… somewhere.

Tammy is also kinda surprised at how 'cool' this nerdy girl everyone ignores really is. She gets kinda angry when she tells me how Grace originally thought Tammy was teasing her and going to do something cruel. According to my daughter, half her schoolmates are 'total dicks.'

Ugh. Kids.

My phone rings.

Hmm. Unknown number. I'm about to let it go to voicemail when a strange urge changes my mind. Maybe I should take this call. Hmm. Swipe. "Hello?"

"Uhh, Ms. Moon?" asks a woman who sounds vaguely familiar.

"Yes?"

"Hi again. It's Heather Carter, Desmond's sister." She pauses. "Did you find my brother yet?"

Ah, okay. "No. I haven't been able to give him the documents. He's proving to be fairly elusive."

"Figured," she grumbles. "Look, he's home right now. He and his buddies always order pizza on Wednesday afternoons. They have like this thing about weekly poker meetings or something. Maybe fantasy sports. I don't know what they do, just that they've been religious about getting together on Wednesdays for years at my brother's place."

"Hmm. Okay. Thank you for letting me know. Worth checking out."

"You're welcome." She makes an odd noise part growl, part sad. "Des needs help. I really think he's going to hurt somebody one of these days. His friends don't see it. They think him grabbing a knife and taking a swipe at them is normal."

"Wow, okay. Well, I'm only a PI serving documents. Not a cop. Not going there to arrest him."

"I understand. Just hoping this court thing ends up with him being put somewhere he can get the help he needs. He'll probably ignore it, not show up, and end up in jail again. They don't help him there, ya know? God, he's such an idiot some-times."

"Yeah, it's not an easy situation, all right."

"Well, I better let you go. It's almost time for them to be there. Just, figured I'd try to help."

"Thanks."

We hang up.

"Lunch can wait?" asks Tammy.

"We'd have to rush to take advantage of this if it's true." I tilt my phone back and forth in my hand, watching the sunlight gleam off it. "Up to you."

She slows to make a right turn. "Might as well get this over with. We can eat after. Boy, I'm going to order so much food."

"How much?"

"Like *two* hamburgers."

I grin. "Okay, now that's just crazy talk."

Chapter Twenty-nine
Service with a Smile

Tammy pulls over and parks a safe distance from Desmond's apartment.

From here, she can video record me handing him the documents relatively easily while being out of harm's way. Between Heather talking about him being violent and my gut telling me to be careful, I want Tammy to stay back on this one. She's sensing it, too, and has no problem staying with the car.

We sit there on a stakeout for about sixteen minutes before a little Nissan with a pizza place thing on the roof pulls up. That's my cue. I grab the subpoena paperwork from my purse, leap out the door, and run down the sidewalk.

The pizza guy—a later twenties dude with long hair—gives me a strange look as I jog up to him. Oh wow, this guy reeks of weed. He wouldn't smell so strongly to normal people, but my nose is supernatural. I'm practically getting high from being next to him.

"Oh, hi." I smile and hold up the papers. "Looks like we're making deliveries to the same address."

"Cool." He offers a disinterested one-shoulder shrug and proceeds up the sidewalk to the door.

I shadow him, standing in such a way as to be difficult to notice from inside the apartment until the door is open.

Tammy takes up a position a little closer than I'd like across the street. She's got her cell phone up and recording. Gotta love technology. It's much more difficult for people to claim they never got the documents when it's so easy to get video of them receiving said papers.

Much to my absolute shock, Desmond himself opens the door. Guess he really lets his guard down when expecting pizza. Sweet. The poor guy looks like the doorbell woke him up. Baggy unkempt clothing, several days of beard, and shaggy hair also kinda gives him the appearance of someone who's frequently high and not terribly concerned with personal hygiene. Could be just a product of mental illness, too.

Desmond starts to smile at the pizza guy and reaches for the box.

I leap forward—a bit faster than normal humans are capable of—duck around the delivery guy, and stuff the subpoena paperwork into Desmond's hand. He reflexively closes his grip on the object touching his palm.

"Desmond Carter, you've been served," I say. "You're subpoenaed to appear in court."

His eyes bulge. He glares at the papers, then at me... then throws them aside so he can yank a handgun out from under his shirt. He shoots at me, but so hastily he misses, putting a bullet into the dirt by the sidewalk. Pizza guy backpedals while shouting a whole bunch of swear words. Desmond whips his arm around, trying to aim for my face while screaming incoherently. My reflexes give me the speed to duck and grab him by the wrist, forcing his aim way into the air before he can pull the trigger a second time.

Even small handguns are painfully loud at close range without hearing protection.

Another bullet streaks off into the sky.

He tries to pull his hand out of my grip, but isn't strong enough. It's been a while, but old training kicks in. Not that I really need it. Being supernaturally strong makes disarming a gunman while judo flipping him face-first into the sidewalk fairly trivial. Like something straight out of a Bugs Bunny cartoon, I more or less swing him around over my head by his arm and wallop him into the ground. Not *too* hard. My goal isn't death, merely to knock the wind—and fight—out of him. Desmond barks like a kicked goose when his chest strikes pavement. He loses his grip on the weapon. I chicken wing his arm up behind his back and perch on him.

"You a cop, lady?" asks the pizza guy.

"Not anymore. Used to be a federal agent," I say. "PI now. You wanna call 911, please?"

"Yeah, totally." The pizza guy nods, then stares at the thermal carrier he's holding in both hands. "Uhh, what should I do with the pie?"

Wow. This guy has definitely smoked too much weed. "Put it down for a moment."

Tammy keeps recording. A minute or two later, Desmond gets his wind back and starts screaming, ranting, and struggling. I simply hold him down as a small crowd forms in response to the gunshots. It takes the police a few minutes to arrive.

Yeah. My lunch date with Tammy is going to end up being more of a dinner date. This will take a bit.

But, hey. Got the process serve done.

**

We have a nice meal at a little Mexican restaurant.

I feel a little bad excluding Ant and Pax, so we order more food to bring home for them. The Prius smells amazing. Little cars, right? It's going to smell like chicken burritos for a few days now.

"Wow," says Tammy on the ride home. "Some people really go out of their way to dodge process servers, but that guy went way too far."

"Seriously."

She glances at me. "Must have been one heck of a lawsuit."

"Just child support stuff. Nothing bad enough to shoot the process server over." I exhale. "This guy... if his sister is right, has got some mental issues. He's also not a big fan of the government. Some of the stuff she said about him makes him sound like one of those sovereign citizen types. Anyway, the guy wasn't the most rational sort of person. But... his legal problems just got ten times worse."

"Yeah. Glad I was recording that." She shakes her head. "What sort of idiot just shoots at someone like that?"

"He's not an idiot. He's sick."

"And an idiot."

"Maybe. Hard to say." I shrug.

"Ma?" She drums her fingers on the wheel as we come to a stop at a red light. "How can you tell if someone is going to freak out like that when you try to give them papers? You know, without being able to read their minds. How do regular people do it?"

I let my head loll back against the seat. "People can't. Not until it happens. Just need to be ready for anything."

She nods. "Hey, ma?"

"Yeah?"

"You wanna watch a movie tonight?"

"Just us?"

"No. Everyone. Pax, Anthony. Maybe Kingsley?"

"Sure. Any reason why?"

Tammy shrugs, looking a little embarrassed. "Not really. Could just use some good family time. Not often you see your mom shot at."

"I'm not your average mom."

"Still."

"Okay," I say. "Tonight is family time. Officially."

She smiles. "Good."

I sit back in my seat as my daughter drives. Yeah, family time.

Just what the doctor ordered.

Chapter Thirty
Sebastian

The following afternoon, Thursday, I find myself taken by a combination of good mood and sudden inspiration.

Sherbet called last night to let me know they
found a guy fitting the description I got from
Rosannah who owned a blue 1979 Pontiac Bon-
neville. I have no idea what that is other than an old
car, but it matches what she said. He didn't go into
much detail about how he managed getting the warrant for it, but a forensic examination of the car
turned up blood in the trunk. It's at least enough to
get a more thorough warrant for the house and property. I'm guessing the suspect, an unemployed man
by the name of Joshua Greyson, is probably going
to say some wild things to the court-ordered psy-

chologist.

Anyway, since there isn't a vampire involved with the other killings, Sherbet can more or less handle the rest of that case on his own. I did tell him about Rosannah, though. He may or may not associate the teacher's death with this case. Talk about a no-win situation. On one hand, they're blaming a guy for a killing he didn't commit. On the other, they'd have to keep a cold case open no one would ever be able to solve. It's not like Greyson is an 'innocent' man, either. He did murder two people. It's anyone's guess if he'd been nuts all his life and watching Rosannah attack the teacher inspired him to act on his fantasies... or if he'd been otherwise normal and simply cracked upon witnessing a real vampire.

I'm going to say he's probably been a suppressed psychopath for a while. Takes more than watching a vampire kill someone to step across that line of becoming a murderer for the pleasure of it. But what do I know? I'm not a psychologist.

As for my good mood, I'm happy to pick up an old routine—meeting with Sebastian for a bit of sword practice. Stabbing slow moving yetis didn't exactly stress me out, but it gave me enough of a clue my skills could use some brushing up. I'd say it's unlikely I'm going to run into someone trying to kill me with a sword any time soon, but this is my crazy life. As soon as I dismiss that idea, I'm going to be up to my eyeballs in bladed weapon combat.

Seemed like a good idea for me to stay in fighting shape. Besides, it's fun.

"Ahh, Samantha," says Sebastian as I enter the basement of his large mansion. It's still far too bright outside for him to go upstairs. "Right on time. It's good to see you again."

"Good to see you, too." I smile back at him. "How have you been?"

"Rather splendid, actually. Just returned from a visit to London. It was a pleasure to see the old country. I hadn't spoken with Titus since the 1700s."

"Lot of catching up to do." I chuckle. He and Titus are the vampire equivalent of high school buddies who grew up and moved to different countries. Every so often they get together and... um, do whatever it is ancient vampires do for fun.

"Smidge, yes." He wags his eyebrows at me. "Though I dare say your life is more exciting than his. I imagine you've got more stories from the past few months than he has in three centuries."

Heh. "Maybe. Titus is, after all, a monk. He's not exactly a fan of the wild life."

"A fair point." He glances at the rack of swords on the wall. "Shall we see how out of practice you've become?"

I select the same longsword I've been using here for practice from the display. Heh. No wonder. It's almost the exact same shape as I conjured the ice blade into. Guess my subconscious knows what it likes. "Let's see."

He flips a rapier up from the rack, then catches it behind its back when it falls while simultaneously snagging a main gauche in his left hand, itself a small parrying blade. "Shall we begin?"

"Let's," I say, returning the longsword to the rack on the wall. "But first, might you have a glass of water?"

Sebastian blinks, clearly confused. "Water? You are thirsty?" He moves over to a gym bag, reaches inside and comes out with a bottle of water.

"Not quite." I grin, taking it from him. "Like you said, I might have one or two new stories to tell."

I open the bottle, set it on the polished floor...

And summon the ice blade.

The End

Samantha Moon will return in:
Sasquatch Moon
Vampire for Hire #26
by J.R. Rain and Matthew S. Cox
Coming soon!

About J.R. Rain:

J.R. Rain is an ex-private investigator who now writes full-time. He lives in a small house on a small island with his small dog, Sadie. Please visit him at www.jrrain.com.

About Matthew S. Cox:

Originally from South Amboy NJ, **Matthew S. Cox** has been creating science fiction and fantasy worlds for most of his reasoning life. Since 1996, he has developed the "Divergent Fates" world, in which Division Zero, Virtual Immortality, The Awakened Series, The Harmony Paradox, and the Daughter of Mars series take place.

Matthew is an avid gamer, a recovered WoW addict, Gamemaster for two custom systems, and a fan of anime, British humour, and intellectual science fiction that questions the nature of reality, life, and what happens after it.

He is also fond of cats.

Please find him at: www.matthewcoxbooks.com

Made in the USA
Monee, IL
29 October 2022

16805303R00164